THE PRISONER OF SNOWFLAKE FALLS

JOHN LEKICH

THE PRISONER OF SNOWFLAKE FALLS

ORCA BOOK PUBLISHERS

Library and Archives Canada Cataloguing in Publication

Lekich, John
The prisoner of Snowflake Falls / John Lekich.

Issued also in electronic formats.
ISBN 978-1-55469-978-0

I. Title.
PS8573.E498P75 2012   JC813'.6   C2011-907571-7

First published in the United States, 2012
Library of Congress Control Number: 2011942581

Summary: Teenage burglar Henry Holloway is sent to a small community
that tests his criminal resolve.

*Orca Book Publishers is dedicated to preserving the environment and has printed this book
on paper certified by the Forest Stewardship Council®.*

Orca Book Publishers gratefully acknowledges the support for its publishing
programs provided by the following agencies: the Government of Canada through
the Canada Book Fund and the Canada Council for the Arts, and the Province of British
Columbia through the BC Arts Council and the Book Publishing Tax Credit.

Design by Teresa Bubela
Cover photo by Perry Danforth
Author photo by Alex Waterhouse-Hayward

ORCA BOOK PUBLISHERS
PO Box 5626, Stn. B
Victoria, BC Canada
V8R 6S4

ORCA BOOK PUBLISHERS
PO Box 468
CUSTER, WA USA
98240-0468

www.orcabook.com
Printed and bound in Canada.

15 14 13 12 • 4 3 2 1

For Jesper

PART ONE

MY LIFE IN CRIME

ONE

I am writing the story of my life in a notebook I stole from a drugstore. Come to think of it, I stole the pen too. Given this information, there is no particular reason for you to believe that I'm especially honest. But I figure writing things down might be a good start in the trust department. I'm hoping that when you know a few things about me, you might begin to understand how I ended up where I did.

I've decided to try a little experiment. While writing my story, I'm going to be one-hundred-percent honest. You never know. I might even get to like it.

With this in mind, I think it's only fair to let you know my real name right off the bat. It is Henry Thelonius Holloway. Feel free to call me Henry anytime you like. You may think, what's the big deal? Everyone has a name. Actually, in my case,

I have a bunch of different names. I have a student ID card that says my name is Horace Latimer. I have a library card that claims I am Marvin O'Hara. And I have a driver's license that swears I am a legally bonafide driver named Antonio Pastorelli.

I first came across the late Mr. Pastorelli's license while making an unauthorized visit to his former home. With the addition of a few borrowed tools, including an X-Acto knife, a laminating kit and a small picture of yours truly, I was able to make some handy changes to Antonio's former ID. By the time I was finished, the Motor Vehicle Department version of Mr. Pastorelli went from being a seventy-seven-year-old senior citizen to someone who happened to look just like me.

It's not that I'm some big-time forger or anything like that. But with a little knowhow and determination, I was able to alter the original license so that it looks close to genuine if you are casually inspecting it in a reasonably dark place.

Even though I may look a few years older than my age, I am only fifteen. That's one of the good things about being the new and improved Antonio Pastorelli. Thanks to my handiwork, it is a documented fact that Antonio has just turned seventeen and can operate a motor vehicle all the livelong day.

By now you're probably wondering why I have so many different names. Let's just say that it's to my advantage to have as many different names as possible. You should also be aware that I steal a lot more than stationery supplies.

In fact, I have stolen everything from a stick of gum to a 1957 Thunderbird convertible. For some reason, I always think better while I'm chewing gum. And driving.

Mind you, I returned the convertible to its original parking space after a couple of hours of driving around and organizing my thoughts. I even ran it through the car wash and tuned up the engine a bit, since I noticed it was running a little rough. I didn't return the gum. But show me someone who wants their used gum back and I'll show you someone whose company you should definitely avoid.

You know how some people are good at playing sports or solving math equations? Well, I'm good at picking locks and hot-wiring cars. I've also been told that I have a natural ability as a pickpocket. Although, the one and only time I liberated someone's wallet, I felt so guilty that I had to put it right back into the side pocket of the sports jacket in question. I don't mean to brag. But the man on the bus who happened to be wearing the sports jacket at the time never even knew that his wallet was gone.

I wanted to get the fact that I'm a thief out of the way as soon as possible. When people find out I'm a thief, they usually react in one of two ways. They are either totally disgusted or they figure my life is like one of those movies where burglars crawl under laser beams to steal valuable paintings or jewels.

I would like to say right here and now that I've never crawled under a laser beam in my life. Also, I do not steal anything that someone has taken the trouble to hang on a wall. In fact, I am currently restricting myself to stealing only the basics. Given my current predicament, I tend to focus on taking money and food. One thing about living in a tree house? There isn't a lot of room for storing excess merchandise. Plus, it's very easy to draw the attention of law enforcement when you're walking down the street carrying a flat-screen TV.

Lately I've been thinking about concentrating on smaller items. You know, wedding rings, wristwatches or the occasional engraved cigarette box. But it turns out I have a problem taking things that people are sentimentally attached to. I have even tried specializing in digital cameras. But then I'll start scrolling through the pictures of some happy family on vacation in Hawaii or Disneyland, and I'll end up leaving the camera right where I found it. I guess that's one of my rules. No matter how hungry you are, nobody has a right to steal someone else's memories.

Not that I'm making excuses or anything. After all, plenty of people are sentimentally attached to their own personal collection of money. And I take cash just about every time I can find any lying around. Also, I came very close to cutting and eating a slice of an untouched birthday cake once, which is about the lowest thing you can do just before someone else's birthday. Especially when you've just broken into their house.

The only thing that stopped me from cutting into the cake? I couldn't figure out how to slice it without ruining all the pink roses on top. According to the fancy lettering, somebody named Angela was just about to turn nine. Anyway, I didn't want to ruin Angela's ninth birthday. So I never took anything that day. Not even a sliver of cake.

The candles were already stuck in the frosting and everything. It reminded me of when I was about to turn nine, which was just after my mother died. My Uncle Andy ended up buying me an extra big cake that year. But nobody felt much like eating it. I hope Angela's birthday was better than that.

If it makes any difference, I try my best to be a very neat and orderly thief. One of the fringe benefits of being a burglar is that I've developed a genuine appreciation for the hectic nature of modern life. Sometimes I'll enter a house and it will be so messy you'd think it had already been burglarized. If I like the feeling of a particular home, I'll straighten up the place before I leave. You know, make the beds, load the dishwasher. That sort of thing.

In fact, I always try to remember that I'm a guest in whatever home I'm burglarizing. An uninvited guest, mind you, but a guest just the same. If it weren't for the unsuspecting hospitality of the people I burglarize, I'd probably be stuck in some foster home right now.

Remember what I said about being honest? Well, here's one of the most important things you should know: my privacy and independence are very important to me. My biggest fear is that I'll end up eating foster-home oatmeal with a bunch of strangers.

Whatever happens, I want to make my freedom last as long as I can. That's why I'm currently spending the summer in an abandoned tree house. Like the big house next to it, the tree house belongs to the widow of Mr. Pastorelli, the man whose driver's license I now carry. Her name is Evelyn, and she has no idea that I've secretly taken up residence on her property. Since Evelyn gets around with one of those aluminum walkers and doesn't venture outdoors much, I consider her the perfect land-lady for my particular situation. There have been a couple of times when I've had to stay very still while the mainte-nance man serviced her outdoor swimming pool. But that's not so bad when you consider that I get free rent for as long as I can remain under the radar.

I have discovered that Evelyn has a lot of pictures in her house. She is a grandmother a few times over, but her chil-dren and grandchildren never come to use the pool. This fact gives me a very melancholy feeling. So even though Evelyn never fails to leave a spare key under the mat—that's about as convenient as it gets in my line of work—I make it a point never to steal from her unless it's absolutely necessary.

I've used the pool a couple of times late at night. I like swimming alone in the dark. It's one of those feelings that's peaceful and not lonely at all. Of course, I try not to abuse my midnight swimming privileges. The worst thing someone in my position can do is get emotionally attached to a place you may have to vacate at any moment.

It's not that I'm complaining or anything. As a rule, I always try to be grateful for at least one thing every day. For instance, today I'm very grateful that it's summer; it makes my current domestic situation a lot easier and automatically eliminates the whole "Why aren't you in school?" question. I tend to stay very active during the warm weather, which tends to keep me from worrying too much. Let me explain.

For most people, summer is a time of fun and relaxation. They go to neighborhood barbecues, catch an air-conditioned movie or take a vacation to the south of France. But, apart from Christmas, summer is the busiest season of the year for a burglar. In summer, homeowners and apartment dwellers get distracted by the heat. They leave their doors and windows open in order to get a nice cross-breeze going. Or better yet, they leave a ground floor window open while they make a trip to the store to get lemonade or bug spray. While I can pick a wide variety of basic locks, an open window on the ground floor is a gift that I can never resist.

Of course, the beauty of a summer burglary is that most of your potential problems are likely to be outdoors, frolicking in the backyard. I am often envious of such carefree behavior. During the summer, I'm too busy going through open windows to enjoy a backyard barbecue even if I were invited to one. Which I never am. Sometimes the wind shifts and I can smell the drifting smoke from the burning coals in some nearby barbecuer's yard all the way up in my tree house. Man, does that ever make me hungry.

I can hear everyone laughing and having a good time, the way they do at barbecues. It makes me want to drop by unannounced and say, "Hi, there. I'm you're new neighbor from the oak tree just down the street. How about setting out another paper plate?" There are even times when I entertain thoughts of liberating a steak from right off the grill. Or maybe even waiting until dark to liberate the entire barbecue set.

Of course, barbecued steak is a little out of my league these days. Most times I have to content myself with whatever leftovers I can find in a stranger's fridge. I have a couple of cans of chili stored in Evelyn's tree house. But if there's anything that brings on that pesky lonely feeling, it's eating your second-to-last serving of cold chili out of a can.

No matter how hard I try, I can't help getting hungry on a regular basis. That's how I came up with the idea of the Henry Holloway Emergency Fund. The charity that keeps on giving—to me.

In fact, if it weren't for the generosity of my benefactors, I'd probably starve. I should point out that I prefer to think of the people I steal from as my benefactors and patrons. Each and every one of them are making unaware—and totally unselfish—contributions to my emergency fund. I often think that it's too bad I can't leave them an official receipt for tax purposes. I guess they'll just have to settle for my unofficial gratitude.

Some of the cash portion of the Henry Holloway Emergency Fund goes toward the continuing demands of personal hygiene. Thanks to recent events, I'm facing various challenges in the cleanliness department. There are many times when I have to be especially resourceful where my personal grooming is concerned. If I run out of coins for the neighborhood laundromat, I can sometimes grab a fresh T-shirt off the outdoor clothesline from a nearby backyard. I always try to return the garment folded and freshly laundered. But I have to make sure nobody's watching. It would be genuinely humiliating to get caught returning something I stole in the first place.

Of course, some of my basic daily needs are quite easily addressed. Thankfully, there are a few public washrooms within walking distance. It's especially fortunate that there's a condominium complex less than a block away from Evelyn's. The complex has an outdoor pool with an attached bathroom and shower. The shower facilities are locked up at night. But there are no security guards or cameras. So it's usually very easy to hop the low fence, pick the simple lock and clean myself up.

The problem? The condo dwellers are starting to have these summer pool parties that can run until after midnight. It's not a good idea for me to be out on the streets after dark, since that can attract the attention of law enforcement. So lately I have been a little negligent in the soap-and-water department.

You might think this is a tough way to get by. But believe it or not, there are many things I like about living in a tree.

Most of the time, if I'm not feeling too hungry, I'll just lie back on my stolen sleeping bag and chill. I like the fact that you get a much better look at the sky from a tree house. Probably because you're a lot closer to it.

I enjoy looking up at the roof of my current residence and watching the little slivers of blue that peek through the cracks in the planks. I guess some people would complain about having a few gaps in their roof. But I always try to keep in mind that I don't pay rent. Which is very reasonable when you consider that I also have the after-hours use of a regulation pool.

I get my accommodating side from my mother. I never knew my dad, who took off before I was born and could have been quite impetuous for all I know. About the only solid information I have on him is from my mother, who said, "He played the saxophone." When I asked if I should know anything else, she added, "He played the saxophone quite badly."

Thanks to the care and attention of my mother's brother, Andy, I have never been all that curious about my dad. I don't know how my dad would feel about my current lifestyle. But I can definitely tell you that my mother wouldn't be too pleased. When I think about how disappointed she would be, I really miss the days when I didn't have to climb a tree to enter my front door.

The place I am currently calling home is one of those tree houses that's a miniature version of the grown-up house on the same property. There's a peaked roof and glass windows with curtains. But I think I like the view best of all. It makes everything look far away and beautiful. Like nothing bad can ever touch me.

Sometimes, when I catch a glimpse of Mrs. Evelyn Pastorelli in her kitchen window, shuffling along with her aluminum walker, I feel guilty. She's getting a bit forgetful, and I can tell it's starting to worry her.

I must confess that, once in a while, I check on Evelyn using a pair of very expensive binoculars that I liberated back in the days when I was concentrating on procuring valuable merchandise. Mostly, this is just to make sure she hasn't fallen and injured herself. I try my best not to invade her privacy. But sometimes I can't help seeing things that make me feel a little guilty.

Yesterday I watched as Evelyn opened her fridge and stuck her head inside for a long time. I could tell that she was trying to find the grapefruit that was there before I decided to eat it. And when she realized it was gone, there was this scared expression on her face. Like she was thinking, Maybe my daughter is right and I should move to one of those retirement homes where I will never have to keep track of grapefruit again.

I try to make it up to Evelyn by doing little chores around the house when she's out running errands. For instance, I found an old oilcan in the basement and fixed one of her squeaky kitchen cupboards. After she got back, I watched her open the cupboard door and look a little sad. I mean, it was almost as if she wanted the old, familiar squeak to still be there. I guess you can never tell what a person will miss when they get to feeling lonely.

Evelyn has a piano in her house, and once in a while she'll play something with the windows open. She is partial to classical music, which I find very peaceful on a still summer evening. However, I wouldn't mind hearing a little jazz. Mostly because that's the kind of music my mother used to play.

When my mother was alive, she played piano in one of Vancouver's less respectable cocktail lounges. This meant that I spent a lot of evenings with Uncle Andy. My mother was always saying, "I love your uncle. But he has some bad habits." Looking back, I guess her biggest fear was that Uncle Andy would teach me to steal. Sometimes she just couldn't help bringing up the subject out of nowhere. She would come home, stooped over from wearing her heavy piano-playing dress with all the silver spangles, and automatically go into this long speech about how theft was the lowest form of human behavior.

I can never remember my mother actually finishing her speech about theft. Most of the time, she would get a decent start before throwing her arms around me and starting to cry. I would stand there for a while, feeling the spangles of her dress pressing against me and smelling the smoke from a thousand cigarettes. She would hug me tighter and say something like, "I'm sorry, Henry. It's been a bad night for tips." Then she would say, "Just promise me you'll never steal anything." And, naturally, I promised.

Sometimes I lie awake and think about how many times I have broken that promise to my mother. How, you may ask, does a fifteen-year-old end up stealing things if he feels so guilty about it? Well, I'd have to say it all started because of a hot-fudge sundae.

I was seven years old when I entered my first private residence without permission. Up until that day, I was always very law-abiding. Back then, I had no idea how unfair life could be. For example, it never occurred to me that my mother could get cancer from all the secondhand smoke in the clubs she played. But she did, even though she never took a puff from a cigarette in her entire life. That's what she kept trying to explain to the doctors over and over. "You don't understand," she would say. "I don't even smoke."

It was a bad time all around. So one afternoon my Uncle Andy decided to take me out for a special treat. My mom had one of her medical appointments at the clinic and I think he just wanted to cheer me up a little. I'm sure what happened next wasn't planned or even expected. But like Uncle Andy always says, "When opportunity knocks, it's always a good idea to invite it in for a cup of coffee."

My Uncle Andy has always been a little different. For one thing, he never failed to carry a bunch of dog treats in his pocket. Even though he has never owned a dog in his life. When I asked him why, he said, "It's just a little professional tip I picked up from the postman."

I asked if he was a postman. I was always trying to figure out what my one and only uncle did for a living. He seemed to have a steady supply of ice-cream money and no job to go with it, which I found very mysterious.

"No, I'm not a postman," he replied. "Although I do encounter the occasional uncooperative pet in my line of work." Then he looked at me and added, "I am very proud to say that I have never been bitten by a dog in my entire career. Chased, certainly. But never bitten."

For a while, I thought my Uncle Andy might be in real estate. He always took an extra special interest in other people's houses, especially if there was an accumulation of newspapers on the porch. On the way to getting our ice cream that day, I remember telling Uncle Andy that a fireman had come to our second-grade class to talk about his job. "I think I might want to be a fireman someday," I said.

We were walking along a back lane, next to a nice old house, when Uncle Andy said, "See the ladder in that yard, Henry? How would you like to practice being a fireman right now?"

I looked around, like maybe there was some house on fire that I didn't know about. Uncle Andy pointed to a partially opened window on the second floor. "Do you think you could squeeze into that little window if I held the ladder for you?" he asked.

"No problem, Uncle Andy," I replied. Like I said, I was only seven and very eager to test my ladder-climbing skills.

"Okay," said Uncle Andy, quickly leaning the ladder under a window. "I'm going to go around front and ring the doorbell. If nobody's home, I will be back to steady the ladder." Then he looked at me very sternly and added, "Stay right here and don't try climbing the ladder by yourself."

At the time, I didn't realize that by squirming through the window and unlocking the door for my uncle, I was about to commit what the police call breaking and entering (or "B and E" for short). A few years later, Uncle Andy would try to put things into perspective for me. "Since we never actually broke anything, we were only guilty of the entering part," he said.

I don't even remember what we took that day. But I do recall this unique feeling of guilt mixed up with genuine excitement. Uncle Andy made it clear that my first B and E— or what he liked to call my "first E"—was a one-shot deal and that I wasn't to tell my mother. He explained that he was in the business of liberating items from other people's homes. Uncle Andy made it very clear that he did not want me going into the liberation business. But I guess it didn't work out that way.

Ever since my mother passed away, Uncle Andy has been my official guardian. It was his idea to pretend that his friend Cindy was my aunt. They even had a fake marriage certificate made up. Just in case the government wanted proof that I was enjoying what they like to call "a stable domestic environment."

Sometimes Uncle Andy has a problem with stability. For example, he is currently in prison for selling a series of instructional DVDs entitled, *The Happy Handyman's Digital Encyclopedia of Home Repair*. You may ask, "How is going door to door selling instructional DVDs breaking the law?"

Well, technically, my uncle did not actually sell the entire Happy Handyman series. In fact, he only sold the first one, which, while accompanied by a lavishly illustrated booklet, merely covered home repair from A to B. This was perfectly fine, if all you cared about was replacing the filter on your air conditioner or repairing a cracked bathtub. But, as it turned out, a lot of people were interested in the rest of the home repair alphabet.

The trouble was that Uncle Andy only had thirty copies of the first DVD. He had discovered it while breaking into a delivery truck when nobody was watching. Fortunately, my uncle is a rather persuasive salesman. He even managed to sell the DVD to a few people who didn't own computers or TVs. Unfortunately even they got quite annoyed. As the judge put it, "When an individual writes a check for a complete series of DVDs, they have a legitimate expectation of receiving the remaining discs."

Usually when my uncle is in jail, it's only for a couple of months at a time. I've always been able to stay with one of his longtime associates in the house Uncle Andy rented. Unfortunately, most of the associates that Uncle Andy trusts are in jail or out of town right now. Also, thanks to Uncle

Andy's most recent incarceration, he fell behind on the rent and we had to move out of our latest house.

My uncle is under the impression that I am staying with some good friends of Cindy's while she has sublet her local apartment to make some extra cash. He thinks Cindy's friends are a very nice couple called the Hendersons. This is only partially true. Until recently, I was staying with a couple called the Hendersons. But they weren't all that nice. At least not as nice as my version of the Hendersons.

Not that things didn't start out okay. When Cindy went off to learn how to be a professional card dealer, Mrs. Henderson did her best to make me feel at ease. The thing is, I don't think Mr. Henderson was all that keen to have me around. He kept dropping these little hints. Like, "How long is that kid going to keep eating us out of house and home?"

To be fair, Mr. Henderson was dealing with a few domestic problems of his own. He was way behind on the bills and his landlord was getting impatient. I've been around a few rent dodgers in my time. So you'd think I'd recognize the signs. For example, Mrs. Henderson started getting very nervous and apologizing for no particular reason. "I'm sorry, Henry," she said, putting her hand over mine. "Truly sorry."

The next day, Mrs. Henderson sent me to the store to buy a few groceries. When I came back to the apartment, I could tell something had happened as soon as I put down the bag.

You end up experiencing a lot of different emotions when you spend time in strange houses. After a while, you sense certain things as soon as you get inside. Like when a place is vacant or when someone's on vacation. There's just this empty feeling that comes over you.

Of course, now and then, the feeling is totally wrong. So the first thing I did at the Hendersons' was check the closets and the drawers. Except for a few hangers, the closets were empty. And all the drawers made that hollow sound you get when there's nothing left inside. I looked around for a note. But I couldn't find one anywhere.

I sat down to think for a while. Since I had no place else to go, I would have stayed in the apartment for as long as I could. But I heard someone coming down the hall. Then I heard a man's voice. It was the landlord, talking to a couple of other people.

Thankfully, the apartment was on the ground floor. So I just opened a window and climbed out as quickly as I could. I heard the key in the lock as I was making my way out. I didn't even have time to grab the bag of groceries. The good news? By the time they were inside, I was already running across the courtyard.

After I finished running, I figured out a few things. I knew I was never going to see the Hendersons again. Just like I knew Cindy wasn't going to call back and check up on me. It's not that they didn't care, exactly. It's just that they got caught up in their own problems and concerns. When they did, other things—like taking care of someone else's kid—kind of fell through the cracks.

When I was a little kid, I remember asking Uncle Andy why my mother had to go away and never come back. He put his arm around me and said that life was like this big magic trick that nobody could figure out. "This is the way it works," he said. "One day somebody's here. And the next day they're gone. It's not your fault, Henry."

"But they're still gone," I said.

"That's right," said Uncle Andy. "They're still gone."

TWO

Ever since my mother died, my Uncle Andy has done his best to look after me. I'm not saying he doesn't have his faults. But I have watched him try to be a totally good person, even though it is clear to just about everyone that he has no natural talent for it. It's funny how you can feel so close to someone, even though they are far from perfect. But that's exactly the way I feel about my uncle.

For better or worse, I take after my uncle in many ways. Like Uncle Andy, I have never been able to say no to a challenge. Of all the weak spots in my character, the weakest is that I can never resist a bet. No matter how foolish. Someone could say, "Henry, I will bet you five dollars that you can't eat a hotdog while standing on your head," and I would automatically have to prove that I can.

One of the things I like best about my uncle is that if I said I could eat a hotdog while standing on my head, he would back me up one hundred and ten percent. He is constantly bragging about how I'm some sort of boy genius.

It all started with the special intelligence test they gave me back in elementary school. I was eleven years old when they put me in this room with several people whose job it was to test me on different things. I scored way higher than anybody my age without even trying, which my uncle has never forgotten. When I started to show some natural curiosity about burglary, he said, "What do you want to know that for? We have documented proof that you are smart enough to become a lawyer and steal the legal way."

Of course, life with Uncle Andy always had its ups and downs. But I really miss the ups. In fact, the thing I miss most is that we used to live in a real house. It was only a rental, and it looked a little sad from the outside. The paint was flaking a bit and a few of the porch steps were loose. But the best part was, it always felt like home.

I'm sure some people would consider my former living arrangements rather unusual. I mean, not everybody has the unique privilege of living under the same roof with an assortment of small-time crooks. But that's where my Uncle Andy was thinking ahead. The beauty of this arrangement?

Even when he was being temporarily detained by the judicial system, there was always someone to look after me.

You can't always count on a steady income from breaking the law. Sometimes things go your way and sometimes they don't. So Uncle Andy would often take in boarders from among his various associates. Rent was always what my uncle liked to call "very democratic." If you happened to be doing well at the moment, your rent was high. If you were down on your luck, your rent was practically nothing.

It is a well-known fact that responsibility can be very exhausting. That was the great thing about living in the same big house with a lot of irresponsible people. On their own, they would let a lot of parental-type things slide by. But as a group, there was always at least one person who could handle feeling responsible for a short period of time. When they got tired, somebody else usually took over.

You would think that a bunch of lawbreakers on the premises would be nothing but trouble waiting to happen. But nobody ever stole so much as a matchstick under our roof. It was considered very bad manners to steal from your own place of residence.

If you were going to live in our house, you had to obey a strict set of rules. Of course, when I was a little kid, I wasn't supposed to know what the rules were. After pulling my first heist with Uncle Andy at the age of seven, he tried his best to keep me from the details of the burglary business. Of course my natural curiosity got the better of me.

So it wasn't long before I discovered that the house rules were posted in everybody's room but my own.

I think it is a sensible set of rules, especially if you ever find yourself living under the same roof with an assortment of burglars and con artists. So I've decided to list them below.

- Should you encounter any problems with law enforcement, do not give them this address.
- No stealing on the premises. (This means YOU!)
- No talking about stealing in front of Henry.
- No swearing or coarse language in front of Henry.
- You will be expected to perform at least one domestic chore per week. (Feel free to let Henry see you doing this.)
- Should you fail to perform said domestic chore, you will be required to help Henry with his homework.
- If you do not feel qualified to help Henry with his homework, you must go to the library and select a book you feel he might enjoy. (Do not steal the book.)
- Family game night is mandatory. (Unless professional obligations intervene.)

My favorite rule of all was the one about family game night. Uncle Andy made this rule because he didn't want anybody to sit in their room and brood or mope. To encourage what my uncle called "wholesome social interaction," he came up with the idea of having a game night every Friday.

He got his hands on some old-fashioned board games. You know, games like Monopoly, Sorry! and Clue. You might not think that grown men would relate to games like that. But you would be very wrong. It wasn't long before they were all playing Sorry! or Monopoly with unabashed zest. Everybody would shout and laugh or ask me to blow on the dice for good luck. It was a lot of fun.

I tend to look back on those more innocent days with a lot of affection. For one thing, I had learned to be independent at a very early age. I had my own room and never had to share anything unless I wanted to. As long as I kept my grades up, and did my share of the household chores, I was treated like a reasonable facsimile of an adult.

There were other benefits as well. You would be surprised at how many things you can learn from living with an assortment of small-time crooks, things that have nothing to do with avoiding the police. Some of these things can even be enlightening when it comes to understanding human nature.

For example, I've always found Wally Whispers attitude very inspiring. Wally's real name is Walter Gurski. But everybody calls him Wally Whispers because he can't talk above a whisper. I asked him why he was unable to raise his voice, and he said it was because of an unfortunate encounter with a very angry individual. "I cannot elaborate any further," explained Wally. "I do not wish to alter your viewpoint on the basic goodness of human nature."

That's Wally for you—always very considerate. The reason he started teaching me how to pick locks is because I was in the habit of forgetting my house key. As a result, I would often have to wait a long time in the rain before Uncle Andy showed up. I started to complain to Wally that Uncle Andy wouldn't let me leave a key under the mat. But Wally said that hiding a key outside your home was a very bad idea. "It is like having a neon sign on your doorstep that reads *Please steal anything you consider valuable.*"

Then there are all the clever devices you can buy to hide a spare house key outdoors. "You can put your key inside a fake plastic rock that looks quite authentic from a certain distance," Wally explained. "Also there is an outdoor thermostat with a hinge that opens up to miraculously reveal your key."

"That sounds very clever to me," I said.

"Oh yes, such gadgets are extremely clever," agreed Wally. "Except for the fact that house burglars peruse the very same catalogues as the people who want to hide their keys."

Wally suggested that it would be way smarter for me to keep a skinny little tool called a lock pick buried in the flowerpot next to the front door. That way, I would not have to leave a spare key lying around for someone else to find, and I could always use the pick if I forgot my key. "Listen carefully to my instructions," he said, "and you will never have to stand in the rain again."

At first, I felt quite guilty about learning how to pick a lock. But Wally said it was just like learning survival skills in Cub Scouts. "You know how they teach you to rub a couple of sticks together and make a fire because somebody forgot to bring matches?" he asked. "Well, this is practically the same thing. Only usually much less hazardous than playing with fire in the woods."

Wally would never admit it, but I think he was proud to be teaching me what he knew about locks. "When it comes to challenging a young person's coordination and mental agility, your computer games and your Rubik's Cubes are child's play when compared to picking a sturdy lock," he said.

It wasn't long before Wally began to brag to the others about my lock-picking abilities. "This kid has the touch," he would say. "He is going to become a big-time surgeon, if the concert violin doesn't get to him first."

Of course, some of Uncle Andy's associates doubted my talent. That's how I started participating in a series of friendly wagers. For example, when I was ten, they asked me to try and open a locked door without using the key. Instead of a key, I was given a lock pick. My uncle and his friends placed their bets and put a pile of cash on the table. I was told that if I could pick the lock in under three minutes, all the money on the table would be mine. I opened the door in under two minutes.

After that, a number of Uncle Andy's friends began to take a personal interest in my development. Before long,

I learned the fundamentals of how to forge an ID, hot-wire a car and pick somebody's pocket on a crowded bus.

None of my uncle's colleagues ever encouraged me to use such skills for financial gain. They were just showing off to me a little. In the words of Mr. Cookie Collito, who can hot-wire anything on wheels faster than it takes to butter a piece of toast, "If we were farmers, we would teach you how to grow corn. But we are not farmers."

Almost all of our boarders in the rented house were men around my Uncle Andy's age. The one exception was Madam Zora, who made her living as a professional fortuneteller in a downtown tearoom. She would forecast people's futures by looking at the lines on their palms or turning over special cards with drawings of things like skeletons and devils on them.

When she wasn't working, Madam Zora let me call her Cindy, which was her real name. She said that people would never believe somebody called Madam Cindy could accurately predict the future. Cindy always seemed to have time to help me with my arithmetic or bake brownies for the class party on Valentine's Day.

You may think that it's impossible to predict the future. But Cindy said that her real job was making her patrons feel good about themselves. She'd always make sure that a customer's future looked very bright, telling them they were going to come into some unexpected inheritance or find their one and only true love. Then she would tell this long, sad story about how her little brother was trapped in a child-labor gym-shoe factory in outer Bulgaria and how she was trying to save up enough money to send him a plane ticket to Vancouver.

At least seventy percent of the time, her customers felt so optimistic about their new and improved future that they'd insist on giving her some extra money for the plane ticket. There was no actual little brother in outer Bulgaria. There was just Cindy herself, who was putting aside a little nest egg so that she could live her lifelong dream of getting a fresh start in Las Vegas.

Personally, I think Cindy was kind of sweet on my Uncle Andy, who I noticed always got the biggest piece of her homemade lasagna. Of course, my uncle is the sort of person who avoids romantic attachments at all costs. When Cindy figured this out, she lost a lot of her initial interest in me. Not that I blame her at all. Everyone deserves a fresh start in life. And she stuck around way longer than I thought she would.

I have visited Uncle Andy in prison a couple of times since moving into the tree house. In his last conversation with Cindy, he learned that I was moving in with her friends the Hendersons. On my last visit, he was very concerned that Cindy was not returning his phone calls.

"She's probably very busy doing her homework for blackjack school," I said.

"Why isn't she answering?" asked Uncle Andy. "She knows how hard it is to make a long-distance call from prison."

For those of you who have never made a phone call from jail, it is very difficult. Your time is strictly limited, and there's always a long line of people pestering you to hurry up and finish. According to Uncle Andy, there's very little privacy. "People are always pushing and shoving to over-hear any news from the outside," he says. "Last week a guy dialed a telemarketer by mistake and ended up ordering a set of commemorative dinner plates."

As it turns out, Uncle Andy's phone situation is working to my advantage. Cindy didn't provide him with a lot of details concerning my living arrangements. So I was able to make my version of the Hendersons sound a lot more ideal than they actually were. Once I got past the lying part, it was actually kind of fun making up my own family.

The pretend Mrs. Henderson was always supervising Girl Scouts or going to charity bake sales. I put a lot of thought into creating my own best friend—the totally fictional but ever-obliging Ricky Henderson. I even made up a cat named Ginger, who is always rubbing up against Ricky's leg and making him sneeze.

My only problem is that Uncle Andy keeps wanting to talk to the Hendersons. I gave him the number to a pizza place that I happened to know off the top of my head. And then I managed to convince him that I copied the number down wrong. He's tried phoning the new number a couple of times, but all he got was a recorded voice that said,

"We're not home right now, but leave a message after the beep." I have no idea who recorded the message. But I'm personally very grateful that it wasn't more detailed.

I should mention that Uncle Andy can always reach me in an emergency, because he's provided me with a prepaid cell phone. We like to call it the Holloway hotline. I carry the phone with me wherever I go and always remember to charge it up whenever I make a trip to the library. He's managed to call me a couple of times when I'm chilling out in the tree house. I'm always very glad to hear from him. Until he asks to speak to one of the Hendersons. Then I have to create a diversion. This usually involves food.

The highlight of Uncle Andy's week is the night they have Salisbury steak. The steak is always served with over-cooked peas and undercooked potatoes. This should give you a good idea of how bad the food is in jail. So, whenever I need to distract Uncle Andy, I conjure up an elaborate menu. "The Hendersons are fine," I might say. "Last night, we had fried chicken with glazed baby carrots and garlic mashed potatoes." And then, just to make the lie sound a little more convincing, I'll add, "Ginger ate a carrot off the floor."

There will be a slight pause at the other end. And then Uncle Andy will say, "The guys want to know what you had for dessert."

"Raspberry crumble," I say.

And then I'll hear a voice in the background saying: "Ask him if it was à la mode."

And Uncle Andy will say, "Did you have ice cream with it?"

"French vanilla," I reply. Usually, after that, I'll have to hang up. Because my stomach will be growling so loud, I'm afraid Uncle Andy will be able to hear it over the phone.

Luckily, my uncle's schedule doesn't allow for many calls. In fact, the most important rule about the hotline is that, while he can call me, I can never call him. "I don't want to be one of those guys who is always waiting for the phone to ring," he says. "If there's an emergency, just make sure the Hendersons call the Warden's office right away."

When it came right down to it, Uncle Andy's attitude toward the Hendersons was very similar to the way most people feel about fake ID. Just about everyone expects you to be exactly who you say you are. This means you have an automatic head start in the deception department. I could tell that my uncle really wanted me to be staying with a good family. So he was all prepared to be convinced, despite a few rough spots.

Don't get me wrong. It's not that I enjoy lying to my uncle. Okay, I'll admit that I don't want him to find out about my little summer adventure. Much as it would pain him, he wouldn't hesitate to turn me over to Social Services if he discovered I was on my own. But it's also a very important bonus for me to provide him with a little peace of mind.

After all, we're family. That means he worries about me and I worry about him. Since Uncle Andy knows that

I worry, he tries his best to put my mind at ease by making jail sound like it is one big recreational center. He has painted me many pictures of horses and dogs over the years, and he has spent so much time doing jigsaw puzzles that he can assemble a three-thousand-piece puzzle faster than any four people working as a team.

Currently he's working on a very complex nature scene entitled The Majesty of Cape Cod. This puzzle demands a great deal of concentration. Which is another reason not to trouble him with the details of my predicament.

Uncle Andy whispers a lot during our visits. He calls it "doing a Wally." My uncle whispers because our meetings take place in a large room called the visitor's lounge. Of course, the average lounge does not have guards. Or fellow inmates who like to eavesdrop because they're so bored. On the plus side, the walls are a nice restful shade of green. And sometimes my uncle is so glad to see me he even forgets to do a Wally.

Every once in a while, when I visit, my uncle likes to pass the time by telling me elaborate stories about his daily life in jail. I think this is because he wants to discourage me from following in his footsteps. He says many of his cellmates snore or talk about gourmet food in their sleep. He says it is impossible to get any rest when someone you are sharing accommodation with keeps mumbling about roast duck with orange sauce.

According to my uncle there is no privacy in prison at all. For example, sometimes Uncle Andy gets help on his puzzles from Clarence, a very big inmate who likes to look over my uncle's shoulder whenever he is busy trying to relax. The most irritating thing about Clarence is that he likes to pester my uncle during his precious puzzle time. "Are you sure you've got that piece of tree bark in the right place?"he might ask. I can tell my uncle is more than a little annoyed at having his jigsaw judgment questioned. But, since Clarence has what he calls "a slight problem with anger management," Uncle Andy cuts him a lot of slack.

Every now and then, a helpful Clarence offers to make a certain piece of the puzzle fit by forcing it into place with his fist. Uncle Andy patiently explains that the whole point of the exercise is to find the one and only piece that naturally fits in that particular space. And then Clarence says, "I'm just letting you know we have another option."

Sometimes, during a visit, my uncle will shoot me a secret look. It's a look that silently asks how much I would like to have Clarence looking over my shoulder and offering to flatten little pieces of cardboard into any shape I want. "Do you think I am smart?" he asks.

"I think you are one of the smartest people I know," I always reply.

"Well, if I'm so smart," says Uncle Andy, "what am I doing in jail?"

The question always gets a big laugh from my uncle's fellow inmates. But then, after a while, the laughter stops because everyone is in exactly the same situation.

I try not to worry too much about Uncle Andy being in jail, but I always do. I also worry that he'll catch me lying. There was something about my last visit that made me especially nervous. Sometimes my uncle can tell that I feel guilty about something, but he's not exactly sure what it is. Finally, he said, "You've been breaking into houses and making up the beds again, haven't you?"

I just looked down at the table, taking a sudden interest in a carved heart that read *Hughie and Laverne Forever*. I could hear him saying, "I know you want to pay back the Hendersons for their kindness. But I'm working on that, okay?" And then he sighed and added, "How many times do I have to tell you? Don't steal."

"Why not?"

"Because as a thief, you make an excellent chamber maid," he whispered.

"I have never been caught," I whispered back, immediately regretting the statement since my poor uncle was currently as caught as you could get.

He took a deep breath and appeared to gather his thoughts. "I started in the business when I was about your age," he said. "Believe me, you won't be able to hide behind being a kid forever." He pinched the sleeve of his orange jumpsuit and asked, "You think it's fun looking like a human Popsicle all day long?"

I didn't have the heart to tell Uncle Andy that I was going through some lean times burglary-wise. Lately, the only money I could count on consistently came from looking underneath the cushions of strange couches. In the world of thievery, there is probably nothing lower than a sofa-change bandit.

Uncle Andy looked like he was reading my mind. "I know it's tough out there without family, Henry," he said. And then, brightening up a little, he added, "Thank god for people like the Hendersons."

Sometimes I think it was a mistake to tell Uncle Andy about my criminal activities. I believe he spends a lot of time feeling bad about not being around to steer me away from a life of crime. He has always thought that if we could buy a place of our own in some faraway town with a really good school, both of us could get a fresh start. He's earned a little time on the prison computer for purposes of self-improvement, and he always uses it to check out the latest real-estate listings.

He fantasizes about buying property in a high-end neighborhood with lots of trees and grass. "There's a whole room for me to spread out my jigsaw puzzles," he says, "and nobody is looking over my shoulder except you."

Then he'll sigh, and I know he's worrying about me again. Last time, he told me why. "You suffer from an overabundance of character, Henry," he said. "What you need to be a successful crook is a definite lack of character."

When I told him that my character would diminish with time, the professional burglar in him looked somewhat hopeful. Then his shoulders began to droop. "It's no use," he sighed. "You're too much like your mother." My uncle thought for a second and then smiled wistfully. "Your mother was the most solid citizen I ever knew," he said. "She couldn't even steal from somebody she disliked. Which is a good thing because she spent her whole life disliking nobody in particular."

I pointed out that there were lots of people I disliked. "Who?" asked Uncle Andy, like it was some sort of challenge. When I couldn't name anybody, he said, "I'm beginning to think I should have turned you over to Social Services for your own good."

I could feel myself getting pale at the mention of Social Services. I guess Uncle Andy noticed. He made me promise to stop breaking into houses while I was living with the Hendersons. It was an easy promise to keep since the Hendersons were long gone.

I was just about to leave when my uncle called me back. "Henry?" he said. "I'm kind of glad you don't dislike anybody."

I could tell that Uncle Andy was missing me, which made me miss him too. That's when I started to get that lonely feeling again, even though my uncle was right there in front of me. I couldn't think of much to say that wouldn't make things worse. So I asked, "How's your puzzle going?"

"It's a funny thing," he said. "Putting together the blue sky is hard because it's all one color. Even so, I think it's my favorite part of the whole puzzle. You know what I mean?"

"I think so," I said. And then I made my way toward the first of several doors that would take me outside. Along the way, I couldn't help but wonder what it would be like not to be allowed to see the sky whenever I pleased.

Sometimes I can't help thinking how different my life would be if I came from a family of farmers. For example, I doubt that Uncle Andy would be incarcerated right now if he had been growing corn. But, like Cookie said, we are not farmers. When you're a thief, the closest thing you have to a barn is called prison. Of course, there is one big difference: Nobody ever leaves the barn door open in prison.

THREE

Sometimes I think that my uncle sits in prison and worries about what my mother wanted for me. In fact, sometimes I think he worries so much that not even Salisbury steak night can cheer him up.

A few years ago he thought he had my future all figured out. Remember that intelligence test I took back in elementary school? After I finished the test, there was a follow-up report with a bunch of recommendations. The testers thought I should go to a special boarding school for really smart kids called the Monroe Academy.

The Monroe Academy was in Victoria, on Vancouver Island. A long way from my uncle or any of his associates in Vancouver. If that wasn't bad enough, the school seemed superstrict.

I've always had a problem following other people's rules. It's not that I'm lazy or anything. It's just that if I'm going to do anything that involves actual effort, I want it to be my own decision. When I read some literature on the school, right away I knew it wasn't for me.

On the front of the academy's brochure, there was a picture of a big gray building with a Latin motto on the front. The English translation of the motto read *To Love Learning Is to Love Discipline*. On the inside of the brochure, the school promised to mold academic warriors in the bracing atmosphere of a Spartan existence. Photos showed their world-class rowing team, a live-in dormitory with rows of tightly made bunk beds and a cafeteria with vending machines for three kinds of vitamin-enriched bottled water.

Boys in shiny shoes, gray flannel pants and blazers featuring the Monroe Academy crest were pictured doing homework, mopping floors and pruning rose bushes for the camera. One guy was so proud to be pruning rose bushes in his blazer that he was almost smiling.

When the testers said they could get me a scholarship to the Monroe Academy as part of the school's program for disadvantaged youth, Uncle Andy called a family meeting with just the two of us.

"I've been thinking about your future," said Uncle Andy. "And I demand that you attend the Monroe Academy."

This sounded strange because my uncle never demanded anything of me. But all I asked was, "What does this place sound like to you?"

"Like prison with neckties," said Uncle Andy. "But that's not the point. This is an opportunity for you to rub shoulders with a class of people I'd be lucky to rob."

"Did you tell them my mother played the piano?" I asked. "No way I'm disadvantaged."

"I agree, Henry. It's not you personally that's disadvantaged," said Uncle Andy. "That's the beauty of the way these people think."

When I said that I didn't understand, my uncle explained that the academy considered him a highly negative influence. "I've already done all the heavy lifting for you just by being me," he said. And then, sounding almost as if he were proud of it, he added, "Don't you see, Henry? I'm your disadvantage."

I was beginning to get a sick feeling in the pit of my stomach. "How often would I get to see you?" I asked.

"Once a year at Christmas," he said, explaining it was part of the deal for my full scholarship. "That's if I can stay out of trouble, which both of us know is highly unlikely."

"I'm not going," I said. "I don't trust any place that makes you get in a rowboat when you're not even trapped on a sinking ocean liner."

"You don't understand," said Uncle Andy, shooting me his most serious look ever. "I'm not giving you a choice."

"So you want me to become some slave in gray flannel pants?" I asked.

"Yes," said Uncle Andy, not batting an eye.

That's how I ended up enrolled at the Monroe Academy for the beginning of grade eight. Right away, I did everything I could to get expelled. I got on the rowing team and rowed in the wrong direction. I cut all the roses off my personally assigned rose bush until there was nothing left but a sick-looking stump. But it was no use. The warden—who called himself the head-master—told me I could not do anything he hadn't seen before.

So naturally, I started escaping. After the first couple of attempts, they locked me up in a private room with another student who was supposed to stand guard. Luckily, my personal guard was practicing very hard to make the track team. So he kept falling asleep. Much to my good fortune, I had managed to steal a tiny crochet hook from tapestry weaving class. After a little bit of experimenting, I found I could pick a lock with the hook a lot easier than I could weave a tapestry.

I escaped five times in the first month and a half—twice going so far as to hide in a van full of empty water bottles that took me all the way back to Vancouver. Unless you count tearing the crest on my blazer while running through the rose bushes, the only bad thing that happened to me was that I kept getting caught and sent back.

After my fifth escape attempt, the headmaster brought in Uncle Andy for a chat. It wasn't long before my uncle started to criticize the academy's lax security. "How do you expect the kid to stay put when your locks are a hundred years old?" he asked the headmaster. Then, almost as if he were bragging, he added, "My nephew could crack this old tin can of a place blindfolded."

"What do you suggest?" asked the headmaster, whose tone was very sarcastic. "Barbed wire? A straightjacket during study period, perhaps?"

Uncle Andy smiled politely. "The kid's always been handy with wire cutters," he said. "The straightjacket's not a bad idea. But I think Henry would find a way to wiggle out eventually. He's always been on the nimble side."

The headmaster offered my uncle a reluctant smile. "I have no doubt that Henry would agree to be shot out of a cannon if it was pointed in your direction," he said.

Uncle Andy asked him to leave us alone so that we could work things out. The first thing I asked was, "Are you trying to get rid of me?"

"You're kidding, right?" said Uncle Andy, who sounded totally amazed.

"I know I get in the way sometimes," I said. "It's not like you asked to be stuck with some kid."

My uncle looked at me for a few seconds. "You can think anything else you want about me," he said, his voice getting very quiet, "but don't you ever think that I want to get rid of you. You understand?"

The thing is, I did understand. My uncle is not someone who says "I love you" all the time. He doesn't even say it once in a while. You might think that he didn't care whether he loved anybody or anybody loved him back. But at that moment, I looked into his eyes and saw everything we'd always meant to each other. I knew he was going to take me out of the Monroe Academy and bring me home. For better or worse, we were family.

I still think it was the right decision not to attend the academy. Believe it or not, there are many things my current lifestyle can teach a person about the human condition. They are the sorts of things you don't learn studying Latin or Greek in a room full of dusty books.

Don't get me wrong. Before my current predicament forced me back into my old habits, I felt pretty good about leaving theft behind. On the other hand, I can't deny that burglary has certain educational benefits extending well beyond my program of cultural enrichment. You may find this hard to believe. But aside for the ability to purchase things like concert tickets, I didn't care much about the money.

In fact, sometimes I ended up taking nothing at all. I didn't really see myself as your typical neighborhood burglar. I even made up my own totally unique job title: domestic anthropologist. Someone who liked to explore the undiscovered places in every strange house. Places with secrets that could leave me happy or sad. Or feeling so bad about somebody's tucked-away troubles that I just had to take out the garbage or sweep the floor.

I remember this one patron named Shirley. She kept this diary all about how she could never find the right person to be with. Back then, I would often take a few minutes just to snoop if there was time, and I ended up reading Shirley's entire diary. It was full of questions like *Is it me? Am I that hard to love?* I felt so bad for her that I practically cleaned her whole house.

After that, I vowed never to read anything private or personal again when I was an uninvited (or even an invited) guest in someone's house. Shirley's diary made me think of something Uncle Andy said when he was warning me about the dangers of looking into other people's desks and medicine cabinets. "I've never robbed anybody who doesn't have one or two secrets tucked away in a private place," he said. "And sometimes that secret's a lot more complicated than where a person hides the key to their front door."

I try to keep this advice in mind. I do allow myself to take a good look at anything that's out in the open. Grocery lists, messages on kitchen chalkboards. That kind of thing. I call this "my postcard rule." Just about everybody will read a stranger's postcard, because the writing is there for everyone to see. Even the postcard writer knows this.

Of course, even when you're trying not to, sometimes you can't help discovering private things about a certain benefactor. When this happens, I always try to look on the bright side. Sometimes the secrets I discover about my benefactors help me to be extra considerate.

Take Chester Hickley, a patron of mine with very special needs. Chester suffers from all sorts of pesky skin irritations. He even keeps a note on his fridge that reminds him to do things like avoid direct exposure to the sun. Last time I was at his place, I noticed he'd dropped the appointment card for his allergist on the kitchen floor. I didn't hesitate to pin it back on the fridge using a magnet that said *Do not forget to...*

To be honest, the professional side of me was making a mental note to stop by again while Chester was out explaining his latest rash to the doctor. But just because you are stealing from a person doesn't mean you can't also be concerned about their health.

It is important for the conscientious house burglar to remember that all benefactors are individuals, with their own peculiar tastes, desires and lifestyles. I always take the time to look at bulletin boards, wall calendars or messages tacked on the fridge. This allows me to keep a mental file on the schedules of all the generous contributors to the Henry Holloway Emergency Fund. Like the day of the week they go grocery shopping or when they have their regular appointment with the hairstylist.

Of course, I try not to get too carried away.

Every steady relationship has to be based on a certain amount of trust. While it may sound funny, this is especially true of a burglar and his most cherished targets. If you want to drop by on someone more than once, you have to have enough faith in the future of that relationship not to steal too much at one time. It's always been my feeling that what you lose in cash and merchandise, you make up for with the comfort and security of familiar surroundings.

For me, this means stealing just enough to make the effort worthwhile but not so much that my patron becomes highly security-conscious all of a sudden. After all, what is the good of having a favorite benefactor if they suddenly decide to turn their home into a bank vault with furniture?

You want to know something else? One of the fringe benefits of inviting myself into a strange home is that, when I least expect it, it leaves me feeling grateful to be exactly who I am. For instance, I will be in the middle of a burglary, glance at a piece of paper tacked to the fridge and suddenly appreciate that I don't need a prescription for high blood pressure or a recurring rash. Another funny thing. It's gotten so that I can immediately tell when I am breaking into an unhappy home. Even before I open so much as a drawer.

I might notice that there are no family pictures on the side table. But usually I'll just get this strange feeling all of a sudden. It's almost as if sadness or loneliness can seep its way into the walls. Like cigarette smoke or the smell of last night's microwave dinner. It's the kind of thing that really makes you appreciate your own home. Even if that home no longer exists.

The thing is, once you open a drawer, you never know what you're going to find. I have always tried to restrain myself from checking out private belongings that have no monetary or nutritional value. That means I make it a strict rule to stay away from such temptations as personal letters or the insides of medicine cabinets. Probably the worst thing I can imagine is reading someone's private correspondence and having them catch me at it.

I would say that ninety-nine percent of the time I'm very respectful of a patron's privacy. My one big remaining weakness is family photo albums. If an album is open on the coffee table, I'll take a minute to look at the pictures when I really should be looking for cash. Before you know it, I can get sentimentally attached to the people I'm robbing. There are certain patrons that I try to steal the minimum from because I'd be genuinely sad if they decided to change their personal security habits.

Once I was making an unsupervised visit to the home of Mr. Ambrose Worton. Ambrose is one of my favorite benefactors. I've visited his place a grand total of three times. Like Mrs. Pastorelli, he's one of those absentminded individuals who likes to leave a spare key close by. You know, under the doormat. Or, if he's feeling especially creative, buried in the seeds of a birdfeeder.

There are some houses you'd never want to visit more than once. But right away I found Ambrose's place very welcoming.

His place is very homey. It makes me want to leave every-thing as undisturbed as possible. Plus, a quick look at the prescription on Ambrose Worton's kitchen bulletin board showed that he suffers from high blood pressure and should not be unnecessarily upset by things like open drawers and scattered papers.

You can tell a lot about a person by what's in their fridge. And Ambrose's fridge always featured an unusually thoughtful selection of cold cuts. I felt so comfortable at his house that, on my second visit, I stopped by for a sandwich and didn't even bother to steal anything.

After a couple of visits, I got to know Ambrose's personal history quite well. According to a card he left right on his desk, he was a member of a single dad's support group. I could tell he was very attached to his only daughter, Melinda, a pleasant-looking teenager who appeared to be around my age. There were pictures of the two of them all over the house. Ambrose and Melinda on hiking trips. Ambrose helping Melinda with her exploding volcano science project. Personally, I found it very heartwarming.

I discovered that Ambrose was the sort of guy who attached little yellow sticky notes to everything as reminders to himself. For example, there were a couple of sticky notes attached to the envelope full of money I found buried under a stack of shirts in his dresser. One of the notes made it clear that the money was intended for Melinda's high school graduation present. The other note had all these calculations on it, showing how far Ambrose had to go before he could afford the bracelet Melinda wanted.

I guess I should have taken the money. When you think about it, is pretty much my professional obligation. I considered this option for so long that I had to make myself a second sandwich. On the other hand, it was clear that Ambrose still had quite a way to go before achieving his financial goal. So I decided that I would take a few dollars out of my own wallet and add it to the envelope. You may think this is weird for a burglar, but it made me feel good.

You'd be surprised how good I can feel when hunger or the fear of getting caught by Social Services isn't getting the better of me. I get plenty of fresh air and exercise. Best of all, nobody tells me what to do.

As a bonus, Evelyn's tree house gives me a bird's-eye view of the entire neighborhood. This is a very convenient method of keeping tabs on the habits of any possible patrons. The view of my potential benefactors has been greatly enhanced ever since I managed to steal the previously mentioned expensive pair of binoculars. Lately I've been keeping tabs on a man I like to call "The Colonel."

The Colonel is a retired army guy who has the kind of bristly crew cut that makes his head look like the business end of a brand-new toilet brush. He lives with a small army of cats he has named after famous military leaders. For example, one cat is named Custer and another is named Napoleon.

There are even two cats named Omar and Bradley, in honor of the famous World War Two general. Even though the Colonel has over a dozen cats, I suspected he might make an excellent contributor to my emergency fund.

I always like to get a closer look at a benefactor's premises before doing any actual burglarizing. Sometimes I pretend I'm selling magazine subscriptions. This usually gets me a quick peek at the layout of the living room. When I first visited him, the very talkative Colonel told me that he already had more than enough magazine subscriptions to periodicals like *Soldier of Fortune, Guns&Ammo* and *Cat Fancier Monthly.* After he informed me of his part-time job as "a mall enforcement official," he introduced me to a few of his cats, including General Patton, who the Colonel said was specially trained to be "an attack cat." As if to illustrate the point, General Patton made an impressive attempt to shred the bottom of my jeans with his razor-sharp claws.

The Colonel explained that General Patton got very upset when any stranger attempted to "breach the interior perimeter," which was marked by a series of used tin cans filled with thumb tacks that the Colonel sharpened using a special nail file. The Colonel told me the cans were tied together with twine and strung across both the back and front doorways at ankle level to form homemade tripwires.

The Colonel also bragged that there was a bucket suspended over a doorway by the stairwell. The bucket was filled with the water he soaked his dirty sweat socks in, and it was specially triggered to dump its contents on an unsuspecting intruder as they made their way up the stairs leading to his bedroom.

The Colonel delivered a very passionate speech about how burglars were "a festering boil on the kneecap of the entire human race."

Having watched the Colonel through my liberated binoculars, I have discovered that, while he has no less than three ancient locks on his back door, I could probably pick all three of them while blindfolded. I have also observed that his house is full of very interesting and collectable items. Antique swords, vintage canteens, old-fashioned pocket watches. It's the type of merchandise that I could sell to my shady friend, Lenny. Lenny is a business acquaintance of my Uncle Andy's. He runs a pawnshop that accepts stolen goods, no questions asked. In the distant past, Lenny helped my quest for cultural enrichment by purchasing some of my liberated items for far less than they are actually worth.

Of course, since I'm lying especially low at the moment, I have no immediate interest in the Colonel's antique collectables. Right now I'm much more interested in his impressive stock of canned provisions. While we were talking, the Colonel mentioned that he liked to keep a lot of canned goods on hand in case of an earthquake or a foreign invasion. "Of course, something along the lines of a nuclear attack is unlikely," he pointed out, "but that is no reason to be unprepared."

I thought the old guy must be lonely, because when I expressed interest in seeing his collection of canned goods, he was more than happy to give me a guided tour of his supersized pantry. It was a very impressive sight, especially for someone in my particular situation. I mean, once you got past all the cat food, he had all sorts of gourmet-type things in little cans that you didn't even need a can opener to open. You just pulled on these little tabs. And voila! All of a sudden you had a feast. Oysters, salmon, gourmet soups. Plus some other kinds of exotic delicacies that sounded very French.

As if this wasn't tantalizing enough, the Colonel showed me a lot of emergency equipment that would be just about perfect for my tree house, including a little generator and a battery-powered hot plate with all sorts of handy domestic features. All, according to the Colonel, one-hundred-percent approved by the military for domestic life in the jungle or other unfamiliar terrain. It was almost enough to make me drool.

On the surface, it was very tempting to think of the Colonel as the ideal patron for all my provisionary needs. The problem? To be honest, I found the Colonel more than a little scary. He was always doing calisthenic-type exercises with unopened gourmet soup cans taped to his ankles. This even freaked out the cats, especially Omar and Bradley, who were always ducking under the couch.

Did I mention that the Colonel has a vast collection of nightsticks from his part-time job as a security guard? Did I also mention that he bragged to me about having a Super Soaker water pistol filled with a special bright red dye he'd mixed up in his basement? He called the formula CR-13. The CR stood for Citizen's Revenge. He told me it took him exactly thirteen tries to get the formula just right.

According to the Colonel, CR-13 smelled like a combination of rotten eggs and boiling roof tar. After several experiments on himself, he had determined that the dye was highly resistant to soap and water; he informed me that the lingering odor was "comparable to that of a very angry skunk."

It was going to take a lot of planning to break into the Colonel's house. Especially if I was going to avoid any pitfalls along the way. Fortunately, Wally Whispers taught me more than how to pick a lock: he also taught me a lot about patience.

I missed Wally almost as much as Uncle Andy. There was something about him that always made me want to listen very carefully. Maybe it's because he has a way of making everything he says sound like a valuable secret. "Every disadvantage has a silver lining," he told me, in regards to his soft way of speaking. "For instance, people tend to pay attention when you whisper."

"But aren't there times when you feel like yelling?" I asked.

Wally shrugged. "I have discovered that nothing worth saying above a whisper is worth saying at all."

"What do you mean?" I asked.

"Well, suppose I volunteered the opinion that I consider you a very polite young man," he said. "Would that opinion sound any more sincere in a louder voice?" When I shook my head, Wally looked very pleased. "So what have we learned?" he asked. And then, answering his own question, he added, "Yelling is not only rude but also highly overrated."

I must admit that there have been a couple of times over the last few weeks that I've felt like yelling. If only to get rid of some extra tension that comes with my present situation. Much as I enjoy my freedom, there are times when I get this lonely feeling that won't go away. It can also get somewhat stressful lying to my Uncle Andy about the Hendersons. But when I feel like yelling, I always try to remember that it's overrated.

The thing I wish most of all? That when Uncle Andy gets out of jail, he'll find a house somewhere so that everybody can be together again. Of course, it's only a dream. And sometimes it seems like that dream is never going to happen. No matter how long I wait.

Not that some things aren't worth waiting for. Yesterday I got back from cleaning myself up at the outdoor pool facility down the street. When I returned to Evelyn's yard, the sky was still blue. It was the kind of sky that looked like Uncle Andy had put it all together just right.

I tried to remember that blue-sky feeling as I drifted to sleep that night. I thought about how great it would be if the world were more like one of Uncle Andy's jigsaw puzzles. A place where every piece was made to fall perfectly into place. That way, no matter how bad it got, you'd always know that blue skies were coming your way sooner or later. All you had to do was be patient.

FOUR

Sometimes I like to think back on the days when I didn't have to steal to survive. Back then, I thought of it as "recreational theft." I didn't have to worry so much about the basics because I could afford to use any liberated cash for the luxuries of life.

You might think that I would spend all my ill-gotten gains on frivolous items like junk food and computer games. But just about every penny I stole back then went into what I like to call cultural enrichment and self-improvement. Like matinee tickets to the theater, opera or symphony. Or maybe a special lunch at the type of restaurant where you have to use at least three forks for a single meal. Even though I have fallen asleep at the symphony a couple of times, I enjoy cultural enrichment a lot.

You may ask, "Why would Henry go to an Italian opera in the middle of the day when he doesn't even understand Italian?" Let me explain. I used to feel extra guilty about stealing, because I knew my late mother would not approve of me indulging in criminal activity. Maybe not guilty enough to stop stealing altogether, but way past guilty enough to come up with a guilt-easing plan that kept some of my mother's long-term wishes for me in mind.

My mother loved the arts and, every once in a while, she would scrape up enough money to take me to a play or a concert. "Let's be extravagant, Henry!" she would say. *Extravagant* was one of her favorite words, and whenever she used it, it meant dressing up to go sit someplace for a long time.

I was young and squirmy at the time. But she explained that I would appreciate the experience later on. "I want you to value the finer things in life," she told me. "I love your Uncle Andy, but all he cares about is beer, poker and staying up late to watch old movies on TV."

There are times when I get lonely for my mother and our extravagant times together. That's why going to an opera or a concert that I know she might have liked makes me feel a little closer to her spirit, if you know what I mean. She was always a big believer in savoring life's more elegant moments.

Once, we were passing a display in a store window and she pointed out a very expensive bottle of French perfume called Springtime in Paris. We went inside the store so that a woman in a little black dress could spray my mother with a free sample. Then she laughed and leaned down toward me so that I could smell what she considered the greatest perfume in the world. From that moment on, I always looked forward to the day when I could save up enough to buy her a whole bottle.

I even told my Uncle Andy that I was starting a perfume fund for her next birthday. The trouble was, my mother got pretty sick way before her birthday and had to stay in the hospital. My uncle got this idea to buy a bottle of Springtime in Paris to cheer her up. "Why wait for tomorrow when she can smell good right now?" he asked.

Our plan was simple. "You kick in the money from your perfume fund, and I will make up the difference with a suitable donation," said Uncle Andy. "But if your mother asks, you tell her you bought the whole bottle with your savings. Understand?" Even then, I understood that my mother would not try a single squirt of any perfume bought with the proceeds from theft. I told my uncle he could definitely count on me.

We went to buy the perfume at a fancy department store, and Uncle Andy asked the saleslady for the biggest bottle of Springtime in Paris she had. I took out all my change and put it on the counter. The saleslady was very nice about sorting all the coins. She even made a little joke and asked if the perfume was for my girlfriend. I said it was for my mother.

I'll never forget the way my mother looked when I presented her with the bottle of perfume. She gave me her best smile, and then she looked at me like maybe it was too good to be true. Right away, I knew she wanted to make extra sure that Uncle Andy had not liberated it from a perfume warehouse or some strange woman's dresser. I showed her the sales slip and then topped things off by lying very vigorously about how I'd been saving up for ages.

Normally, my mother would have asked a few more questions. But she was pretty pale and skinny at that point— what you'd definitely call frail. So she cut the questions short to save energy and just smiled. "Why don't you squirt some in the air right now?" she asked, looking at the bottle like it was part of some very nice dream she was having. "You know, like they do at the perfume counter."

"Isn't that a bit wasteful?" I asked.

"What the heck, Henry," she said, a little bit of color returning to her cheeks. "Let's be extravagant."

And so I squirted a little perfume in the air while my mother lay back on her hospital pillow and closed her eyes. She looked so happy that I asked her what she was thinking about. "I am thinking about our lunches at Chez Maurice," she said. I guess of all our extravagant times together, the lunches at Chez Maurice were her favorite.

Playing piano in cocktail lounges didn't leave my mother with a lot of money to throw around. But whenever she could afford it, we would go to a really nice restaurant called Chez Maurice, famous for its delicious French pastries. She would try to teach me the finer points of dining etiquette.

Like which fork to use for salad and how to politely address a waiter. It was her favorite restaurant because, as she put it, the whole place was "glued together with good manners."

Chez Maurice was run by the Girards, a father and son who were both named Maurice. In the busy kitchen, everyone called the son Young Maurice and the father Old Maurice. Old Maurice was the owner and head pastry chef. He was originally from Paris and kept a little replica of the Eiffel Tower by the cash register. Sometimes Old Maurice would talk sadly about growing up as an orphan and the hard times he had in Paris. But he was normally a very jolly individual.

Old Maurice was round all over and had a little gray mustache that looked like it was painted on. He always wore a pink rosebud in the lapel of his chef's jacket and called me *Henri*, the French way to say Henry. Old Maurice always stood very straight. He told me once that he was very proud of his posture. "As a waiter you must always assume that others are paying close attention to your deportment," he said. "Slouching is very bad for business."

You might think that Young Maurice would be a lot like Old Maurice. But he wasn't. Young Maurice was very slim, unsmiling and clean-shaven. Old Maurice described him as "Someone who is inexplicably crazy for rapid exercise and all kinds of fizzy water!" But even though Young Maurice was crazy for exercise, I would often see him slouching while serving customers. Personally, when it came to slouching in the restaurant, I agreed one hundred percent with Old Maurice. It just wasn't the sort of place where anything should look tired or droopy.

At Chez Maurice, the napkins were folded in the shape of swans. So whenever my mother felt it was time to go to the restaurant again, she would say, "Henry, I think it's time that we went to visit the swans." My mother always said the same thing when they put a swan-shaped napkin on each of our plates. "It's so pretty that I can't bring myself to unfold it." Maurice would bring her an extra napkin for her lap. After that, he would place the swan beside her plate so she could look at it all through lunch.

The thing I remember most is how happy my mother was during those lunches. We would laugh and her cheeks would get a little flushed from the single glass of wine she always ordered. Even though I was just a kid, I knew she was the prettiest woman in the room. I think Old Maurice thought so too. He promised that he was going to name a special pastry after her someday. Plus, he always made sure we had table number six, a window table with the best view in the entire place.

Old Maurice came over to our table once and asked, "Does the gentleman find his ginger ale satisfactory?" My mother said, "We're pretending its champagne, Maurice." After that, Old Maurice brought my bottle of ginger ale over to me in an iced champagne bucket. He would say, "Someday, you will grow tall and this will be champagne!"

and we would all have another good laugh. At the end of every lunch, Old Maurice never failed to take the pink rosebud he wore in his lapel and give it to my mother. She never failed to blush and say, "*Merci.*"

Old Maurice reacted the same way every time. His eyes got a little watery and then he gave a little bow. Like my mother was a European princess or something. "No, thank you, madame," he would say. "It is my great privilege to be of service."

I guess my mother never forget how special she felt at Chez Maurice. When she was sick in the hospital, I would squirt some of her perfume in the air and she would say, "Let's pretend we're at Chez Maurice. What are we having for lunch?" In real life, she wasn't really eating much at all. But as soon as she started to pretend we were visiting the swans, she developed quite an imaginary appetite.

After deciding what we were going to have for the lunch we weren't actually eating, my mother would get worn out. It was never hard to tell when my visit was over. Mostly because she would ask me to leave the bottle of perfume on her bedside table. "I just like to know that it's there," she said.

What was my biggest hope? That my mother would get better so we could go back to Chez Maurice. I used to think about her spraying on Springtime in Paris and getting all dressed up. You know, looking just like she used to. But the last time we visited the swans together, it was just in our imaginations.

After Mom died, I took the bottle of perfume off her bedside table at the hospital, and I have kept a close eye on it ever since. I make sure to travel light these days. I have a backpack filled with such essentials as a toothbrush, a few lock-picking tools and my emergency Holloway hotline cell phone. Not to mention a big bottle of Springtime in Paris. I would not confess this fact to just anybody, mostly because of the embarrassment factor, but if anything ever happened to that bottle of perfume, I'd be very upset.

A while ago, I got the idea to go back to Chez Maurice for lunch. It was her birthday and I was feeling nostalgic about the happy times we had there. Also I had saved up all my burglary money and wanted to do something special. This may sound weird, but sometimes I have trouble remembering what my mother looked like. I mean, I'll close my eyes and try to recall the details of her face and everything will get a bit hazy.

I had grown up quite a bit since the last time I was in the restaurant, and I didn't think anybody would recognize me. Young Maurice—who didn't seem so young anymore—didn't give me a second look. But I could see Old Maurice squinting from across the room like he was trying to figure out if it was me.

I could tell he was really glad to see me. He took my hand and started to pump it like he was still a young Maurice. "But it has been so long!" he exclaimed. "Why do you not come to see Old Maurice?" Then he looked around, all excited, and asked, "But where is your dear mother?"

I explained to Old Maurice what had happened to my mother. I told him it was her birthday, and I was taking the whole day away from school to do the kinds of things that reminded me of her.

Old Maurice didn't say anything, but I could tell he was upset. His eyes were starting to water. Then he pulled himself together and got very official. Calling over a waiter with a quick snap of his fingers, he said, "The gentleman will require table number six."

I could hear the waiter whisper that table six was reserved for a larger party. "Move them to table number eight!" ordered Old Maurice.

Even though I ended up sitting at good old table number six, I was kind of confused at first. Despite the fact that I was dining alone, there were two table settings. Naturally, I thought there was some mistake. But the longer I looked at the white napkin swan across from me, the more I understood what Old Maurice was trying to do. If you just concentrated on the swan instead of the empty chair, it was almost like my mother was there. Like she was just in the washroom—combing her hair or putting on a fresh coat of lipstick—and would be back any minute.

Of course, my mother was never coming back to table number six. Old Maurice did his best, sending over a bottle of ginger ale in an iced champagne bucket just like the old days. But eating at a table for one made me sad.

Old Maurice was a little melancholy himself. Apparently Young Maurice wanted to get rid of the tablecloths and swan-shaped napkins and turn the restaurant into one of those sleek, high-tech places that look like very expensive cafeterias. "He thinks I am a useless napkin-folder who is ready for the Old Pastry Chef's Retirement Home!"

We talked about my mother and, after a while, the waiter brought the bill. When I made a move to look at it, Old Maurice snatched it up smoothly from the little bill tray and ripped it in two neat little halves. When I protested, he said, "In memory of your dear mother." Then he took the pink rose from his lapel and placed it on my mother's plate next to her napkin swan.

"Without his mother, a boy's life is like a custard tart without the crust," he observed. "There is nothing to hold it together." His sad eyes got watery again. "If there is anything you need, Maurice Girard Senior is eternally at your service," he declared. He wrote down his home phone number for me before clicking his heels and giving a little bow. "You will remember this, Henri?"

I told him I would and thanked him very much in French. And then Old Maurice headed back toward the kitchen. Even though he was moving for the kitchen at a fast clip, I thought he looked a little tired. But then he straightened up, put his shoulders back and kept moving. I guess he knew that everyone was paying attention to his deportment.

For a minute, I just sat there and looked at the rosebud next to the napkin swan. It gave me a funny feeling, like I was sad and grateful at the same time. You might not think that those two feelings can go together, but once in a while, they really do. I guess that's why I took all the burglary money out of my wallet and left it on the little bill tray as a tip for Old Maurice and his staff.

After my visit to Chez Maurice, I made up my mind to stop recreational theft for good. And you know something? I did stop. Even before I moved into Evelyn's tree house, I was beginning to consider myself more or less reformed. I think my mother would have been proud of me. At least for a little while.

Mind you, there have been a few times lately when I can't help thinking of all the things I could buy with the tip money I gave Maurice if I still had it. But you know something? Ever since my last visit with the swans, I can see my mother's face a little more clearly every time I close my eyes and think of her. And there's no way you can ever put a price on that.

Back when I was still going to concerts, I liked to use what I called the Chez Maurice technique whenever there was an empty seat beside me. I just looked at the empty seat and pretended that my mother was at the coat check or just up the aisle getting a program. Right before the lights would dim, I'd almost convince myself that she was going to return to her seat and tell me to stop squirming and listen to the music.

Sometimes I wonder if all the cultural events I have attended are actually making me the sort of refined individual my mother would appreciate. I guess that's the thing about living by yourself in a tree house. It gives you the chance to reflect on a lot of memories that wouldn't normally cross your mind in a house full of people. Sometimes I'm so busy reflecting that it's hard to get to sleep.

There is a certain time of night when, even though I live in a big city, things get very quiet. Evelyn has stopped playing the piano and gone to bed. There is no *whoosh* of traffic or stirring of branches. Sometimes I will look down and see the pink plastic table and empty little chairs that Evelyn's grandchildren used to play with. On the table, there is a dusty little tea set, just waiting for some long-lost kid to pour pretend tea for Evelyn. When you think about it, nothing feels emptier than a chair that somebody used to enjoy sitting in.

It's funny how the mind works. I mean, I'll look at that empty little chair and I can't help thinking about my mother and the empty chair at table six of Chez Maurice. Eventually, I will start wondering what she would make of my current situation. This wouldn't be so bad, except that I always end up thinking about how much I miss her.

This may sound weird, but when things get really bad, I take out my mother's bottle of Springtime in Paris and spray a little in the air. It doesn't put me to sleep any faster.

But it does make me think of those gentler days with Old Maurice. The days of napkin swans and pretend champagne at table number six. When my mother's chair was never empty for longer than it took to wish she'd come back.

FIVE

Ever since I was a kid, being even a little bit hungry has given me bad dreams. The past couple of nights I've dreamed that a police car was taking me away in handcuffs. Both times I've woken up in the middle of the night in a cold sweat. This is so upsetting that I have to calm myself down by closing my eyes and visualizing the inner workings of various locks. This is a talent I learned during my advance training at the Walter Gurski School of Lock Picking. I find it very soothing during times of stress.

Mind you, the police-car dream is not my only problem. Things haven't been going so great when I'm awake either. Try as I might, I have not been fortunate enough to steal much more than small change. This is disturbing enough as it is. But when I looked out the window of my tree house this morning, who did I see at Evelyn's back door? None other than Mr. Cookie Collito. It was enough to make me graduate to full-fledged panic.

Cookie's real first name is Orville. But he has such a sweet tooth that even the police call him by his nickname. Under normal circumstances, I would be delighted to see him. Cookie is the person who taught me how to drive as soon as my foot could reach the gas pedal. Plus, he has taken me to many enjoyable horse races over the years.

In addition to his passion for sweets, Cookie can never resist anything that's free. He is a dedicated coupon clipper who is always entering contests to try and get something for nothing. When he isn't clipping coupons or entering contests, Cookie is busy stealing.

Cookie specializes in stealing golf carts. He dresses up like an avid golfer and hangs around with a group of guys playing a round. When they are all preoccupied with the game, he drives off with their golf cart. He knows someone who will buy the carts, no questions asked.

Don't get me wrong. Cookie is skilled enough to steal an armored tank if he wanted to. But he says he prefers taking golf carts because of the fresh air and pleasant social interaction.

Cookie has done so well liberating local golf carts that he has been on vacation in Palm Springs, California, for the past couple of months. He sends Uncle Andy postcards about how relaxing it is to actually play an entire round of golf without worrying about the pressures of work. Cookie and my uncle are very good friends. So I knew the first thing Cookie would do when he got back into town was pay a visit to my uncle in jail.

It didn't take me more than a few seconds to figure out that Uncle Andy had sent Cookie around to check out the Hendersons. Cookie is very diligent when given a task. I knew he'd keep coming back to Evelyn's place until he was satisfied that I was in the proper domestic environment.

I should explain that I made the mistake of giving Uncle Andy Evelyn's address when he asked where the Hendersons lived. I always try to tell my uncle a half-lie whenever a whole one can be avoided. But even a half-lie can develop into something totally unexpected.

For example, there was Cookie knocking on Mrs. Pastorelli's kitchen door. Fortunately, Evelyn was at her weekly bridge club meeting. This gave me the opportunity to go around to the front door, get the key from under the mat, and intercept Cookie as if I was an actual resident. Unfortunately, Evelyn was due back from her meeting in just a few minutes. Between my sudden panic and climbing down from my tree house very fast, I was perspiring quite a bit.

Cookie was very pleased to see me and immediately apologized for not being able to take me in himself, since he was currently staying with his cranky cousin in an "adults only" apartment complex.

"Your uncle has requested that I investigate your domestic situation and report back to him," explained Cookie. "Where is Ricky?"

"Soccer practice," I lied.

Then Cookie pulled out a rubber squeaky mouse out of his pocket. "This is just a little something for Ginger," he said, looking around. "Where is she?"

"You know how cats are," I replied. "She's probably hiding someplace."

Cookie put the rubber mouse on the table, sniffed the air and asked, "Do you smell liniment?" When I did my best to look puzzled, Cookie added, "You know, the lotion people use for sore muscles."

"Oh, that!" I said. "Ricky pulled a leg muscle at the last soccer game."

"No kidding? And he still wants to practice?"

"That's Ricky for you," I said. "He's not the bench-warmer type."

"I guess I was expecting something that smelled a little more inviting," he said, sounding disappointed that the smell of baked goods was absent from the air. He looked suspiciously at Evelyn's cold, empty stove and then checked the clock on her kitchen wall. It is a very unusual clock, with pictures of different birds where the numbers should be. Every hour it chimed out a different bird call. But Cookie wasn't very interested in the clock. "Shouldn't Mrs. Henderson be preparing a nutritious lunch about now?" he asked.

"Mrs. Henderson is at a PTA meeting," I said.

"In the middle of summer?" asked Cookie.

"She's very dedicated," I said trying my best to sound casual.

I glanced at Evelyn's bird clock. She was usually back from her card game around the time the blue jay started to squawk, and the squawk was getting closer by the second. Cookie walked over to Evelyn's refrigerator and peered inside. There was a jar of pickles, several cans of sardines, a puckered-up lemon and a carton of milk that was a week past its expiry date. Then he went over to Evelyn's cookie jar, which resembled the head of a smiling pig. He removed the top of the pig's head and pulled out a cookie. "Store-bought?" he said, sounding as if he had just been shot through the heart.

"Mr. Henderson bought a box from the Girl Scouts," I said, hearing a drop of my own sweat plop to the floor.

"This looks stale," he announced tragically. And then— because he can't resist anything that's free or sweet—he popped the cookie in his mouth anyway. "Just as I suspected. I have been incarcerated in places with fresher baked goods."

"You just hit the wrong day," I offered. "Grocery shopping is tomorrow. Plus, Mrs. Henderson has recently sprained her bread-baking arm."

"How did she do that?"

"Loading the suv with a big box of used clothes," I said. "For charity."

"They must be going through a lot of liniment," said Cookie, sniffing the air again. He was staring at me, and I could feel more sweat running down my forehead. "Did you know that you have a twig in your hair?" he asked.

"I've been gardening," I lied. "I like to help out around the house as much as I can."

Cookie looked down at Evelyn's linoleum, like he was feeling guilty about something. "Speaking of being responsible," he said, "I have a confession to make." Cookie coughed nervously. "I owe your uncle some money," he said. "I was supposed to give it to you so you could pay the Hendersons back. You know, for expenses." Cookie was starting to turn pale. "Honestly, Henry. I had the cash," he said. "But now I don't."

Aside from stealing golf carts and being a little too fond of sweets, about the only vice Cookie had was the racetrack. So I asked, "What was the name of the horse?"

"Chocolate Chip," he replied. "I just couldn't resist betting on a horse named after my favorite cookie." Looking very melancholy, he added, "I figured we could double our money. But after the race, all I had left was enough for the rubber mouse."

"I'm sure Ginger will appreciate it," I said. Then the blue jay on the clock squawked; it startled me so much that I gave a little jump. I started to imagine Evelyn coming through the door and finding two strange people and a rubber mouse in her kitchen.

"Just an observation, Henry," said Cookie, "but you seem kinda stressed-out."

"What do you mean?" I asked, as innocently as possible.

"Well, you've dropped a few pounds since the last time I saw you," Cookie said. "In addition, you have these dark circles under your eyes." He pulled the twig out of my hair, adding, "Are you sure these people aren't just using you as their personal gardening slave?"

Cookie ran a finger over Evelyn's kitchen windowsill and examined the thin film of dust. Sounding more like a guidance counselor than a thief, he said, "I am afraid I cannot give the Hendersons a passing grade."

All of a sudden, I forgot about Evelyn and started to imagine being placed in a foster home or some sort of government institution. I started to talk very fast. "I promise that, if you come back next week, you'll be greeted by a well-stocked fridge, a dust-free house and the welcoming aroma of home-baked cookies."

Cookie allowed that he owed me a favor because of losing my uncle's money at the track. "I guess I can stall your uncle until next week," he said, looking at me like I was one of his favorite horses at the racetrack. "But you better be looking well-groomed and rested!" Then he reached into his wallet and insisted I take his last five dollars. "Buy some air-freshener," he said before departing. A minute and a half later, I was in the tree house, sweating like one of the losing horses Cookie always bets on as I watched Evelyn unlock her back door.

I guess maybe Cookie is right about me being stressed-out. Not that I don't have my reasons. My benefactors are being more careful about leaving loose cash around. In some cases, they are also keeping less food in the fridge. As a result, I am being forced to venture into unfamiliar territory more and more often.

Despite the fact that I try my best to be careful, I have experienced an unlucky streak of three narrow escapes in the last few days. The first time, I only got away because my new patron likes to whistle a cheery tune while searching for his house keys.

I did not anticipate my second narrow escape either. To be fair, I did everything according to standard burglary etiquette. I rang the doorbell to make sure no one was home. I even had a story prepared about wanting to hire myself out to do chores around the neighborhood. Just in case someone answered.

Of course, there are some homeowners who prefer not to answer their door while they are at home. They figure it's just some dorky salesman or maybe someone going door-to-door offering personal insight into a particular religion. They could even be sick in bed, which happened to be the reason for my second narrow escape.

I was already inside the house. It was unusually big with a lot of ground to cover between exits. I was thinking how hard it would be to make a quick getaway when I heard a woman call from upstairs.

"Al, is that you?" she asked, sounding like she had a very bad head cold.

Here's another important rule for any aspiring burglar: Do not answer a resident who is calling out from another part of the house. For example, it is never a good idea to reply, "Yes, honey. It is definitely me, the one and only Al." Mostly because you don't know what Al's voice sounds like. I mean, he could have a very heavy Lithuanian accent and how would you know?

Sometimes the homeowner will provide you with a convenient way out of your predicament. For instance, the woman in bed with a cold said, "Al, have you got your nose in the fridge again? How many times do I have to tell you? That leftover chicken is for dinner tonight." I guess Al liked to go into the fridge a lot, because she added, "I better hear that fridge door closing. And I better not hear any chicken-eating sounds after that. If I have to come down there, you're going to be sorry!"

I knew that if she came downstairs, I was going to be twice as sorry as Al would ever be. What if she saw me? I would be in real trouble if she screamed. Even with her cold, I could tell she was probably an excellent screamer. And an excellent scream can cause the worst kind of chain reaction for a professional burglar. The first thing you know, a dog starts barking like there's no tomorrow. Or the next-door neighbor, who keeps a baseball bat in his umbrella stand, decides he needs to check things out.

At times such as these, it doesn't always pay to think like a thief. What you have to do is think like good old Al. I opened the fridge door very quietly, so my benefactor wouldn't hear, and then slammed it shut with a loud *thunk*. I thought if she heard the loud *thunk* from upstairs she would assume that Al was wisely following orders.

Sure enough, she seemed to be comforted by the sound of the fridge door closing. "I love you, Al," she said, before taking a break to blow her nose. "But you are so predictable."

I figured that it was safe enough to carefully make my way out of the house. I was about to do so when I heard her say, "Al, honey, would you run to the store and pick me up a box of Kleenex? There's some money on the kitchen counter."

I put the money in my pocket. It was more than enough for a box of Kleenex. And then I remembered that I had a new packet of tissues in my backpack. Before making a smooth getaway, I took the packet out and placed it on the kitchen table. I hope that—in some small way—it helped her get over her cold.

There's one very interesting thing that I have yet to mention about being in the burglary business. You can be patient, cautious and very smart—all good things for a thief to be—but no matter how careful you are, bad luck is unpredictable. It's like my Uncle Andy always says: "Bad luck has put more clever crooks in jail faster than you can say, 'Do you hear sirens?'"

While Uncle Andy and his associates have many practical skills, they are probably the most unlucky crooks you would ever want to meet. Once I overheard them planning to liberate a bunch of mattresses from a warehouse. They planned the whole thing for weeks, but when they got to the warehouse, it didn't have any mattresses in it. Just plain bad luck.

When I was a kid, Wally Whispers used to tell me all sorts of bedtime stories that he made up. My favorite was about a big-time jewel thief named Wally, who stole a jewel called the Star of British Columbia and lived happily ever after. Whenever Wally told the story, I could tell he was dreaming of a big score. That one final job where he could retire and not have to worry about disappearing mattresses.

Sometimes I fantasize about finding the Star of British Columbia under a new patron's bed. But all I ever seem to find lately is the kind of exercise equipment that promises you a flatter stomach in ninety days. This is bad for both my financial situation and my professional self-esteem.

I keep thinking that maybe it would be a good idea to have some quick extra cash in reserve. Just in case I have to vacate Evelyn's tree house in a hurry. So I decided to stoop to what is probably the lowest form of burglary there is—commonly referred to as "yard work."

To most people, yard work means cutting the lawn or trimming a hedge. But to a thief it means stealing property from people's backyards. Status-wise, yard work is at the very bottom of the burglary food chain. It requires no talent whatsoever because you don't even have to enter the house.

I was so desperate that I stole a couple of outdoor patio chairs from my benefactor, Chester Hickley. I took them to Lenny, that shady friend I told you about. Lenny always says that he doesn't like to get involved in the personal lives of his regular suppliers. And yet, even though he would never admit it, I think he was actually concerned about my welfare. When it came right down to it, Lenny was not that crazy about a minor bringing him stolen goods. He was always trying to convince me that I should be in the library or playing out in the fresh air.

When I came in with the lawn chairs, Lenny seemed genuinely glad to see me. "Hey, Henry," he said. "Long time, no see."

The two of us always got along pretty good. On the other hand, Lenny was a businessman. So he agreed to keep our little arrangement a secret from Uncle Andy. As long as I brought him merchandise that he could use.

"That means no rakes, hoses or watering cans," he said. "And none of those plastic garden gnomes either."

Needless to say, Lenny was not very thrilled with my offer of Chester's lawn chairs. "Yard work, Henry?" he said, sounding as if he'd just been told that his one and only son had to register for summer school. "Is this what you call applying yourself?" Then he looked at me in a very skeptical way and asked, "How am I supposed to sell these?"

I decided to play it cool. "What do you mean?" I asked. "Have people stopped sitting down outside all of a sudden?"

"Let me explain something to you about patio furniture," said Lenny, who stopped unwrapping his lunchtime sandwich to elaborate. "Patio furniture is like hockey or baseball cards. People like to have the complete set."

"What are you saying?" I asked, suddenly distracted by Lenny's sandwich.

"I'm saying that your chairs are worthless without a matching table and patio umbrella."

"But those umbrellas are huge," I protested. "You have to unscrew them from the base. And how do you expect me to lug a whole table down the street by myself?"

"So cut a couple of your little friends in on the action," he said.

"I can't afford friends on what you pay me," I said. "Besides you know I like to work alone."

Lenny rolled his eyes. "Excuse me," he said. "I forgot that you're the lone wolf of lawn-chair theft."

Lenny continued unwrapping a very pungent sandwich that was cut in half. "Of course, this whole discussion could be avoided if you'd just bring me a wristwatch once in a while," he said. Picking up half of his sandwich, he took a big bite and started to chew like it was a job he enjoyed. "Nobody expects a wristwatch to match anything except their wrist."

"What kind of sandwich is that?" I asked.

"It is a concoction of my own invention," explained Lenny. "Sardines, raw onion and peanut butter on pumpernickel." Lenny stopped chewing for a moment and added, "I know it sounds gross. But the more you experience it, the more you appreciate it."

"How much experience do you need?" I asked.

"It depends on how adventurous your taste buds are," said Lenny as he resumed chewing.

I must have been experiencing a severe attack of sandwich envy, because I snapped at him, "Are you going to take the chairs or not?"

Lenny did not get angry. He just squinted at me. I noticed he was staring at a squashed leaf that was stuck to the front of my T-shirt. "No offense," he said, "but you look like you've just come back from a very discouraging trip to the woods."

I was about to answer when my stomach growled loudly. Lenny was looking at me the way I'd seen him look at certain customers who were down on their luck. Elderly types who brought in old cuckoo clocks or porcelain figurines of puppies rolling around in the grass. "Okay," he said. "Against my better judgment, I'll give you five bucks for the lawn chairs. And because of our longstanding professional relationship, I'll throw in the unused half of my sandwich."

"Deal," I said, taking the uneaten half of his sandwich and trying to bite into it as nonchalantly as possible. It tasted weird at first, but I was so hungry that I just kept chewing.

After a couple of bites, I apologized to Lenny for being cranky. "I understand what you mean about the patio umbrella," I said, "but the dermatologist says Chester should avoid direct sunlight."

"No names please," said Lenny. "Too much personal information upsets my digestion."

He watched me eat for a while.

"You know something?" I said. "This sandwich is pretty good."

Lenny sighed. "Okay, ten bucks," he said. "But for that, you're going to have to listen to some free advice."

"Okay," I said. "Shoot."

"Get out of the business, Henry. I'd hate to see you get nabbed for stealing a lawn sprinkler."

"And why would that happen?" I asked.

"Because you're losing your nerve," said Lenny. "And when a burglar loses his nerve, he might as well steal a pair of handcuffs, put them on himself and wait for the police car on the curb."

Personally, my feelings were very hurt by Lenny's advice. But I tried not to show it. I told myself that Lenny was wrong. But tonight I observed a perplexed Evelyn squeezing Ginger's toy mouse. It was almost as if she thought the resulting squeak would tell her what the heck it was doing in her kitchen.

I feel quite bad for making Evelyn think she is losing it. I am also very disappointed in myself. It was the first time

I'd ever slipped up and left something behind in a patron's house. It makes me think that maybe Lenny was right. Maybe I am slipping, burglary-wise.

My stomach lets out a surprisingly loud growl. And I realize that I am feeling hungry again. Have you ever heard that expression *listen to your gut*? It means that you should do what you feel you've got to do without thinking about it too much.

Well, I am listening to my actual gut while trying to listen to my gut at the same time. There is nothing like lying in a dark tree house and listening to your stomach growl to make you wonder what happened to your professional pride. I decide that there was only one thing left to do. Right after I make the decision, my stomach growls again. Just like it is saying, "Go for it, Henry."

SIX

For the next couple of days, I thought a lot about breaking into the Colonel's house and raiding his well-stocked pantry. I had discovered through dedicated surveillance that the Colonel worked the day shift on his security job three days a week, which meant that I could break in during the daytime with very little risk.

Mind you, there is always a price to pay for independence, and right now that price involved coming up with a plan of action for robbing the Colonel. The first thing I did was liberate an expired can of sardines from Evelyn's kitchen cupboard in order to distract the Colonel's cats while I was busy raiding the pantry. Fortunately, this was just about the only advance planning I had to do. Unless you counted working up enough nerve to do the job.

The first part was easy. After picking the Colonel's three ancient backdoor locks fast enough to break a personal record, I felt reasonably stoked about the whole invasion process. Since I had picked a day when I knew for sure that the Colonel was at his security job, the only problem I had to deal with was his army of cats. A few of them were outdoors frolicking around and a couple of them rubbed against the front of my leg as I was about to break into the living room. They were so welcoming that I threw them a couple of sardines.

Of course, I had to be mindful of some of the home-made booby traps in the Colonel's home. I had to gently step over the collection of tack-filled tin cans that were strung at ankle level across the back doorway. After that, it was simply a question of leaving a few more sardines around the living room.

The only cat who wasn't distracted by the food was General Patton, who seemed very annoyed that I had made it past the tin-can perimeter. No matter how much I beckoned with an open can of sardines, General Patton would not stop howling. He even kept howling while digging his claws past my sock and deep into the skin of my right ankle.

General Patton's attack made me yell out in pain. I was just thinking how glad I was that nobody was home, when I heard the Colonel's voice from upstairs calling out, "Who's there?" I must confess I was greatly surprised at this turn of events. He must have been put on the night shift on short notice, or maybe he was sick. Whatever the reason, he was definitely home in the middle of the day. I could feel beads of perspiration on my forehead, and my heart was beating way faster than usual. I could also feel my ankle starting to bleed through my sock.

I hoped the Colonel would stay upstairs if I stayed quiet, but I didn't count on General Patton, who was yowling like a fur-covered fire alarm. I was just about to run out the front door when I saw the Colonel coming down the stairs.

It's funny the things you notice in a highly stressful situation. For example, I noticed that the Colonel was wearing camouflage-patterned pajamas as he inched down the stairs with a nightstick in one hand and—to my horror—a Super Soaker full of CR-13 in the other.

The Colonel and I froze at exactly the same moment. We stood there until he yelled, "You!" and then I ran like heck for the front door. General Patton decided to take a serious swipe at my other ankle, and the Colonel came racing down the stairs looking confused.

A split second later, I was able to understand what the confusion was all about. The Colonel was obviously trying to decide whether to hit me with his nightstick first and then squirt me with CR-13. Or squirt me first and then hit me with his nightstick. To be honest, he was freaking me out.

The good news? I managed to get the front door open. The not-so-good news? I forgot all about the tin cans full of thumbtacks that were strung across the doorway at my feet. I tripped over them, releasing a small flood of thumbtacks before I sprawled across the open doorway. A few upended thumbtacks pierced my jeans and T-shirt. Not to mention one that ended up stuck into the palm of my hand as I floundered around, trying to get up.

Getting assaulted by sharpened thumbtacks is both irritating and humiliating. But it is a walk in the sunshine compared to knowing that an angry individual is about to hit you over the head with a nightstick. Fortunately, the Colonel was so excited at the thought of bashing a genuine intruder that he tripped over a cat toy on the stairs and lost his balance. As a result, he activated the bucket full of dirty sweat-sock water that teetered over the doorway. His total surprise at getting soaked gave me enough time to get up off the floor and run out the door.

And then disaster struck. Before I could get completely out of range, the Colonel fired on me with his specially equipped water pistol. It's hard to describe what it is like to be drenched on the neck and back with the Colonel's special formula just when you think you've made a successful retreat. Especially if you want to be delicate and not use a lot of swear words. Let's just say that the way I smelled wasn't going to remind anybody of Springtime in Paris. Let's just also say that I reeked beyond description.

In fact, I reeked so bad that, even while I was racing out of the Colonel's yard and down the street, I kept wondering why I couldn't outrun this totally outrageous stench. It was only when I slowed down that I fully realized the awful smell was coming from me. That was kind of a turning point, hygiene-wise.

In addition to my lingering odor problem, I had to find a way to prepare for Cookie's return visit to Evelyn's house. That meant tidying up her place, stocking her fridge with healthy food, and convincing Cookie that Mrs. Henderson was baking up a storm. I needed a comfortable place to clean up and tend to my recent scratches and thumb-tack wounds. It should also be a place where I could liberate enough first-class groceries to transfer to Evelyn's fridge in time for Cookie's next inspection.

So I decided to head for Ambrose Worton's place in an effort to refresh myself. Aside from his bountiful fridge, Ambrose's home could easily pass for a health spa. Even without looking inside his bathroom medicine cabinets, I knew it they would be well stocked with aromatic bath salts and soothing lotions, things I desperately needed. His home also featured a number of amenities that made for the ideal stress-free environment: a washer and dryer, and a deluxe reclining chair with a built-in back massager. Best of all, there was a generous sunken bathtub where I could take a good long soak and banish the pesky effects of CR-13.

Normally, I would respect Ambrose's personal schedule by not lingering for much longer than it took to fix a sandwich, but thanks to the Colonel, my nerves were unusually frayed. A personal spa day courtesy of Ambrose Worton was just what I needed.

According to the wall calendar in his study, Ambrose was away on a business trip for the rest of the week, and his daughter Melinda was working as a counselor at a kids' summer camp. Since Cookie's inspection was the following day, the timing was perfect. I could transfer whatever Ambrose had in his fridge and pantry to Evelyn's place. Since Evelyn had a doctor's appointment in addition to her weekly card game, it would leave me plenty of time. If I worked fast, I could even do a fair amount of cleaning before Cookie's arrival. I made a mental note to borrow some of Ambrose's cleaning supplies.

It wasn't an ideal plan. I would have to think of a reasonable explanation for the fact that no Hendersons were around for Cookie's second visit. When Cookie departed, I would have to remove Ambrose's food from Evelyn's kitchen, bring it back to Ambrose's and put the food back exactly as I found it. But it was all doable after a bit of rest and relaxation.

I didn't think anybody would blame me for tending to my wounds with the contents of my invisible host's medicine cabinet. Upon reflection, I suppose I did take a little too much advantage of Ambrose's unintentional hospitality. I figured that, as long as I was washing my clothes at his place, I might as well luxuriate in a nice, warm bubble bath. It seemed only natural to use half of Melinda's raspberry-scented bubble bath.

At first, I was a little worried that my clothes wouldn't get clean in time. Fortunately for me, Ambrose had an impressive collection of big fuzzy bathrobes, including an electric-blue one that still had the price tag on it. I tried it on. It was a little long in the sleeves, but once I got used to the scratchy tag, it was surprisingly cozy. I even found a pair of matching fuzz-lined slippers that were a reasonably close fit.

It felt good to pamper myself. I only had my sleeping bag at the tree house, which did very little to cushion me from the hard floor. So it was a real treat just to soak my sore muscles in Ambrose's tub for a while. I felt so rejuvenated afterward that I decided to bake a few cookies to put in Evelyn's cookie jar. Ambrose had a brand of cookie dough in his freezer that promised chocolate-chip cookies "with that unmistakable homemade taste." They certainly smelled unmistakably homemade to me as they were baking in Ambrose's oven.

By the time I put my clothes in the dryer, the cookies were done. I put them out on a big plate to cool. A couple of bags of Ambrose's groceries were packed away in one of his extra suitcases. All ready to go. There was even a little cooler for perishables that fit snugly inside the suitcase.

Even though Ambrose and Melinda were not due back that night, I planned to leave well before dark. Ambrose had his lights on an automatic timer, and his immediate neighbors would be coming home from work before too long. If one of them knew Ambrose was away and spotted me moving around, it could mean trouble.

But I had to stick around until my clothes were dry—that's when my natural curiosity came in. On previous visits I had figured out that Ambrose has a little trouble sleeping. I knew he had a sleeping mask that was designed to blot out any excess light and relax your tired facial muscles at the same time. He also had a special relaxation CD that was supposed to lull you to sleep with the peaceful sounds of a babbling brook and chirping birds.

I ended up sitting back in Ambrose's recliner, wearing his sleeping mask and listening to his relaxation CD. I could feel my stress melting away faster than a pat of butter on a hot piece of toast.

The CD was playing and the clothes dryer was humming, and it was so soothing that I drifted off into the best sleep I'd had in quite a while.

I guess that's why I never heard the key turning in the lock. By the time I heard the door swing open, it was too late to escape. In a funny way, it was a relief that I couldn't see anything through Ambrose's sleeping mask.

Of course, even though there was still a lot of humming going on, I could hear the *thunk* of a dropped suitcase and a man's shocked voice. "What are you doing in my bathrobe?" it sputtered. "In my chair! Wearing my sleeping mask!"

I could tell the man was very upset. Mind you, I was a little agitated myself. On the other hand, I figured it was best to stay calm. I turned off the chair's massager and then pushed myself forward so that I was sitting upright. I took off the sleeping mask, even though I already knew who was there. He looked just like the guy in all the photos. Only way more stunned. "Careful, Ambrose," I said. "Remember your blood pressure."

Ambrose was listening to the sound of my clothes spinning in his dryer like he'd just heard some very disturbing news on the radio. Hoping to relax him, I asked, "Would you like a cookie? They're fresh out of your oven."

A shocked Ambrose picked up a cookie and took a bite, probably because he didn't know what else to do.

"I guess Melinda's still at camp, huh?" I said.

Ambrose swallowed his bite of cookie before he spoke, which I thought was very polite under the circumstances. "Excuse me?" he inquired in a very squeaky voice. "But do I know you?"

"Not exactly. But I know you," I said. "Sort of." That's when I decided to explain my situation. Fortunately, Ambrose was quite fascinated by my story. Especially the part where I added money to his fund for Melinda's graduation present.

"That's a relief," he said. "To tell you the truth, I thought I was going a little batty."

I apologized for making Ambrose question his mental state. He took it very graciously. In fact, Ambrose was so interested in what I had to say that he drank three glasses of milk and ate five cookies while I talked. I could tell that he was warming up to me, in spite of the fact that I had broken into his residence and made myself right at home.

Ambrose was even kind enough to point out that I had not made a professional mistake by misreading his calendar. "I was able to come home early from my business trip," he told me. "If I had stuck to my regular schedule, we would never have met."

Things were going so well that I thought there was a chance Ambrose might let me go. But as it turned out, he was a big believer in following the rules. I briefly considered shoving Ambrose out of the way and taking off in his electric-blue bathrobe, but it's very hard to shove somebody after you've had milk and cookies together. Especially when the person you are thinking of shoving is wearing a milk mustache and asking you to recommend a better hiding place for his spare key. "But I'm the one breaking into your home," I pointed out. "I'm not supposed to know where your key is."

"I never thought of it that way," said Ambrose. "Thanks, Henry."

In the end, I let Ambrose call the authorities. Partly because I thought I'd end up in jail anyway if I wandered the streets in his bathrobe, but mostly because I didn't want to put Ambrose through any more stress. He was very nice when the police arrived—shaking my hand, wishing me luck and asking if my clothes were dry enough. He even sounded a little guilty when he told me that calling the police was for my own good.

This may sound weird, but I was actually relieved to get in the back of the police car. The arresting officer was very nice when he put the handcuffs on me, explaining that it was nothing personal and he was only following regulations. Now that it was true, at least I didn't have to dream it anymore.

I calmed myself down by closing my eyes and imagining that I was picking the lock on the handcuffs. I could probably have done it too, if I'd had enough time and exactly the right tools. But what would be the point? Not even the smartest thief can get out of a locked police car.

With my background, I figured I was going to get a one-way ticket to some sort of prison/foster home. On the other hand, I wouldn't have to lie to Uncle Andy or Cookie about living at the Hendersons anymore. And I would get regular meals and access to a bathroom. But while there are a number of things a person could think about while they are in the back of a police car, all I could think about was how much I was going to miss my imaginary family.

I suppose that sounds a little strange, since we are talking about the kind of family that never existed in the first place. But I had gotten attached to them anyway—or at least the idea of them. And I knew for sure that—wherever I was going—it would not be at all like the picture of domestic bliss I created with the Hendersons.

At least, I thought I knew some things for sure. But it turned out I didn't know anything for sure at all.

After I was arrested, I stayed in a temporary foster home for a while. I had to experience everything I don't like about temporary foster homes. Strange people, strange food and a series of even stranger people from Social Services asking me personal questions. The less said, the better. I was planning my escape when something unexpected happened.

I was sent to hang out for a few days with an elderly gentleman named Judge Horatio Barnaby. I mean, I moved right into his house for a few days so that he could "observe" me. All I took with me was my usual small backpack of essentials, including my lock-picking tools and the Holloway hotline cell phone, both hidden in a special secret compartment that I had constructed myself by cutting into the lining and sealing it over with some Velcro.

Judge Barnaby had a very nice place, not like prison at all—unless you counted the fact that I wasn't allowed to leave. Mind you, since the locks at Judge Barnaby's were extremely pickable, there was what you might call ample opportunity for escape. On the other hand, I was very curious about why I was staying with Judge Barnaby. I also appreciated that the bed in his guest room provided an excellent opportunity to hone my sleeping skills.

Judge Barnaby was retired, with all sorts of diplomas displayed on the walls of his home office. He wouldn't tell me much about what was going on at first, but he asked me all sorts of strange questions. For example, he played bits of music from various opera CDs and asked me to identify the operas. I did quite well, thanks to mom's insistence on cultural enrichment.

Also, Judge Barnaby asked me if I could play anything on the grand piano that sat in his living room. Fortunately, Uncle Andy had insisted that I take piano lessons on those rare occasions when he could afford it, so I managed to fake my way through one of my mother's favorite songs—"Brush Up Your

Shakespeare" by Mr. Cole Porter. I even knew the lyrics, which are very humorous and made Judge Barnaby laugh quite a bit.

In my experience, people rarely lie to you when they are happy. That's why it's always a good idea to ask someone an important question while they are in a jovial mood. With this in mind, after I finished the song I looked at Judge Barnaby and asked, "Am I going to jail?"

"Jail?" Judge Barnaby laughed, as if the question were ridiculous. "Whatever gave you that idea?"

"Well, if I'm not going to jail, where am I going?" I asked.

"You're going to a town called Snowflake Falls," said Judge Barnaby.

"What if I don't want to go?" I asked.

Judge Barnaby was very accommodating when it came to clarifying my options. "The choice is yours," he said. "It's either Snowflake Falls or some form of correctional facility that I fear will clash with your unique personality."

He pulled out my surprisingly thick file. "I don't know how you managed to fall through the cracks with so much documentation on you," he said. "It's really quite a tribute to your exceptional avoidance skills."

Judge Barnaby turned his attention to my file, the one that got me temporarily sent to the dreaded Monroe Academy. "The report states that you're one of the brightest subjects tested in recent years," said Judge Barnaby. "It also states that you have a problem with following rules and schedules you don't agree with."

"I don't like being told what to do," I admitted. "Or when to do it."

He nodded. "Quite so," he said. "I also have a rather extensive report from the headmaster at the Monroe Academy. He says you climbed out of a third-floor window using the rope normally reserved for Tug-of-War."

"That was after they took away my crochet hook."

The judge laughed again. "Ah, yes," he said. "The crochet hook incident."

"How come you're so interested in me?" I asked. "I'm just your average underage thief."

"You may be a thief and you may be underage," said Judge Barnaby, "but there's nothing average about you." He pulled out a single sheet of paper from the file. "A few days ago, I received this from Mr. Ambrose Worton. It's a very persuasive letter pleading that we be lenient with you."

"That's very considerate of Ambrose," I said.

"I think it's more than considerate," commented the judge. "What interests me is why a man you have robbed repeatedly would speak up so earnestly on your behalf."

"We bonded over milk and cookies," I explained.

"Mr. Worton mentions that you actually added some of your own money to a sum of cash found in his drawer?"

"Most of it was money I stole from other places," I confessed. "I wasn't returning it or anything. I was just sort of recycling it."

"You know, for someone so schooled in dishonesty, you can be refreshingly straightforward." Judge Barnaby laughed again. When I asked what was so funny, he apologized. "It's just that you're so perfect for the program," he said.

"The program? What program?"

"I run a unique program that's had some success with, well, people like you." The judge cleared his throat before continuing. "It's called Second Chances. We give certain special cases an opportunity to turn their lives around by moving them to less urban communities and placing them in the care of appropriate families."

"It sounds like Witness Protection," I said. "You know, like I'm running away from the Mafia or something."

"Nothing as glamorous as all that," he replied. "What we really want you to do is experience an ordinary domestic life for a change."

"What about my Uncle Andy?"

"We can arrange for limited, supervised visits once your uncle finishes his sentence. Both of you would have to put in a formal request." The judge looked at me very seriously. "This is just my opinion, Henry. But I think it would do you a lot of good to be apart from your uncle for a while."

"How long will I have to live in Snowflake Falls?" I asked.

"Anywhere from four to six months," he answered. "It could be a shorter stay, if you violate your probation in any way."

"That means I'll be there until Christmas at least!" I took a deep breath and tried to stay calm. "What will happen to me after my time in Snowflake Falls is over?"

"A committee decides what to do with you based on your performance in the program," explained the judge. "It's unlikely you'll be going back to your uncle. At least for the foreseeable future."

"But where will I go?" I asked.

"That's up to you," said Judge Barnaby. "The committee may suggest placing you in a more restrictive environment."

"You mean like one of those jails for underage offenders?"

"A youth detention facility is an option, Henry." The judge smiled encouragingly. "Of course, my hope is that we'll be able to place you in long-term foster care after your time in Snowflake Falls. At least until we can take a close look at your uncle's ability to make some serious changes in his lifestyle."

"But isn't your program just another way of sticking me in a foster home?"

"Second Chances operates a bit differently. I know the people you'll be staying with," said the judge. "The Wingates are just what you need."

"But you're paying them to look after me, right?"

Judge Barnaby nodded.

"How bad do they need the money?" I asked.

"They're not doing this just for the money, Henry," he replied. "Of course, things are a little slow in town at the moment."

"How slow?" I asked, thinking I might be able to catch up on my sleep.

"Don't worry, Henry," said the judge. "We'll find plenty for you to do. In fact, we've worked out an entire schedule of activities for you."

"Why are you sending me to this place?"

"Think of it as a necessary shift in perspective," said the judge.

"But I don't want to shift my perspective," I said.

Judge Barnaby sighed. "Change is hard, isn't it, Henry? Did you know that you're my last Second Chancer? After we see how things work out for you, I'm retiring from the program and going fishing."

When I said I hoped he caught a lot of fish, the judge looked at me kindly and told me not to steal anything in Snowflake Falls. "There are people there whose job it is to keep an eye on you and send back written reports."

"You mean like secret government spies?" I asked. "Snowflake Falls sounds like a great place."

I don't think Judge Barnaby appreciated my sarcasm. "I'm handing you a genuine opportunity, Henry," he said. "Don't waste it." Then he added, "Besides, you might find Snowflake Falls more surprising than you expect."

"What's so surprising about it?" I asked.

"Nothing." And then he thought for a second and said, "Nothing and everything."

"I don't get what you mean," I said.

"You will," said the judge. And then he began to laugh all over again.

PART TWO

WELCOME TO SNOWFLAKE FALLS

SEVEN

Right after my mother died of cancer, Uncle Andy said that life is the biggest con artist of them all. I think he was trying to tell me that just when you think your future is going one way, fate will hand you a surprise that is virtually guaranteed to knock you on your butt.

I was reminded of this on the way to Snowflake Falls, a town on northern Vancouver Island that was stuck somewhere between too small and officially midsized. Way back when, there was a very busy pulp and lumber mill in Snowflake Falls, but it was barely operational now, and a lot of people had moved away.

When I googled the town's name on Judge Barnaby's computer, it didn't look like I'd be able to keep up with my program of cultural enrichment. I mean, there was no opera company and no restaurant like Chez Maurice. A lot of the businesses were only open a few days a week. I don't know if you could call the town sleepy. But it sure seemed to take a lot of naps.

It just didn't look like my kind of place. Of course, I figured that I wouldn't be staying there long, since my plan was to escape as soon as possible. Unfortunately, Judge Barnaby had anticipated this, which is why he gave me my own personal escort to Snowflake Falls. His name was Leon Tully. Even though he was wearing cargo shorts and a T-shirt that read *I Love Texas Hold'em*, he was definitely an official government youth worker. You know, the kind of twenty-something guy who was paid to relate to wayward juveniles such as myself. In spite of his youth, Leon had already escorted a few other Second Chancers to Snowflake Falls, and while serious about keeping an eye on me, he was also very chatty. He talked quite a bit while driving to the ferry. The first thing he said was, "I've read your file, Henry. I gotta say, I'm impressed."

When we were on the ferry and I asked if it was okay if I went to the washroom, Leon said, "I'm afraid it is my sworn duty to accompany you to the facilities."

"You're going to go with me to the washroom?" I replied. "I can't believe it!"

"Boy, that's really good," said Leon admiringly. "The way you sound genuinely indignant and all."

"I am genuinely indignant."

Leon explained that he almost lost his last Snowflake Falls escort when the guy tried to climb through the window of a gas station mens room on the way to the ferry. "And he wasn't nearly as escape-prone as you." Leon grinned at me. "So shall we answer the call of nature?" he asked, like we were going to hit the buffet table together. "If you use the stall, please make sure that your feet remain on the floor at all times."

I had a sudden picture of Leon watching my feet in the toilet stall and decided I didn't have to go to the washroom after all. This didn't seem to bother Leon, who was very upbeat. "As soon as I deliver you to your sponsor family, I get to return to actual civilization," he explained. "I have discovered that the most exciting thing about Snowflake Falls is the well-paved road out of town."

"I wouldn't mind a little boredom," I said, trying to look on the bright side of things. "It sounds rather peaceful."

Leon actually snorted. "Peaceful? You won't get any peace staying with the Wingates."

Of course, I wanted to know more. Fortunately, Leon felt that there was no harm in giving me "an officially unofficial briefing on the Wingates." He made me swear to keep it just between us. Then he leaned over and whispered, "If you ask me, I think it's cruel to leave a guy totally unprepared for the Wingate experience."

"So what are they like?" I asked.

"Well, there's the dad, Harrison Wingate," said Leo. "He owns Wingate's—the town's oldest department store. It's been in the family for generations."

"So?"

"So lately he's been all stressed-out because a new Biggie's has moved in across the street."

"Biggie's Bargin Barn?" I said. "They sell everything there is to sell."

"Everything from barbells to barbecues," agreed Leon. "Dirt cheap too." Leon began singing the Biggie's jingle. All about how Biggie's was "cheap, cheap, cheapest because we're big, big, biggest."

I got him back on track by asking, "How many kids do the Wingates have?"

"Only two," Leo said. "But after a while it's going to seem like a lot more." He shook his head in wonderment. "There's Charlotte, who's this book-crazy brainiac. She's eleven, and she reads instruction manuals for fun. She's gonna wanna run your entire life."

When I asked how Leon knew this, he laughed. "Because Charlotte wants to run everybody's life," he said. His eyes widened. "She actually tried to give the last guy in your situation a haircut. And she has no barber training whatsoever."

Leon's eyes started to glaze over so I had to nudge him along. "You said there were two kids?"

"There's Oscar. He's almost three." Leon rolled his eyes. "The good news is, he keeps to himself and doesn't talk much."

"What's the bad news?"

"He screams."

"A lot?"

"Oh yeah. I think it's a weird form of communication. One of your predecessors said there seemed to be a wide variety of screams that only the family could understand. You know, like one scream for milk and another for cereal."

"That sounds awful."

"Plus, there's a rumor that the kid bites," said Leon. "I haven't seen any actual teeth marks or anything, but the last guy in your position was pulling a double shift at Top Kow Burgers just to keep outside Oscar's bite zone."

"What's Top Kow Burgers?" I asked.

"Pretty much the social center of Snowflake Falls," said Leon. "Unless you count the new Biggie's."

"Wait a minute," I said. "Top Kow Burgers is the big fast-food chain, right? The one where the cow is wearing the top hat?"

"Yeah, that's the one," said Leon. "Anyway, where was I?"

"The last guy, pulling a double shift?" I said.

Leon nodded gravely. "He said he'd rather mop the floor at Top Kow Burgers for the next six months than listen to one more scream from Oscar."

"What happened to him?"

"I think Charlotte developed a little crush on him," confided Leon. "After a few weeks, he was practically begging to be tossed in jail." He leaned toward me and whispered, "For the Wingates, that makes three straight Second Chancers who never actually stood a chance. They have the worst record of any sponsor family in the program."

"So why are they still allowed to take people in?" I asked.

"Harrison's a good friend of Judge Barnaby's," explained Leon. "The Wingates really need the extra money that the program provides. You know, what with the new Biggie's sucking the life out of their business and all. The Wingates need you as much as you need them," he said. "If you don't stick it out for the whole program, they're going to be cut off." Leon looked at me sympathetically. "Knowing you're their last chance might give you some leverage. It's just something to remember when you can't stand it anymore."

"Thanks, Leon. I really appreciate it."

"Yeah, well, you should have seen what Charlotte did to the last guy," he said. "I wouldn't wish that haircut on a bank robber."

We got off the ferry and began the drive into Snowflake Falls. I noticed that it was quite a hike from the ferry terminal into town. Escape on foot would be difficult. Of course, I'd have to put any thought of escape on the back burner. Leon had given me a lot of other things to think about. We didn't speak again until we were just outside the entrance to town.

There was a big wooden sign that looked like it had been carved by a giant lumberjack. It read *Welcome to Snowflake Falls Where.*

"Where what?" I asked Leon.

"I don't think they've made up their minds yet," said Leon. "The town council's been trying to think of a slogan for ages. I hear they're having a contest to find a saying that best captures the spirit of the community. I've been thinking of entering." It was hard to miss the sarcasm when he added, "But I guess 'Welcome to Snowflake Falls Where Nothing Much Ever Happens' isn't the best way to attract tourists."

In a few minutes we were on the main drag of Snowflake Falls, where we got out of the car to stretch our legs and take a look around. At first glance, the hub of town seemed like a bunch of tired-looking buildings huddled together for mutual support. At second glance, you couldn't help but notice a lot of peeling paint. "Things were a lot more prosperous around here before the pulp mill went to a three-day week," explained Leon. "Someone told me there even used to be a video arcade way back when."

Even though it was the middle of the day, there were only a few people on the street. I was about to point this out when Leon said cheerfully, "Man, it's really busy this afternoon. The hardware store must be having its closing-out sale."

"You mean it doesn't get any busier than this?" I asked.

"Well, there's Pumpkin Fest coming up in the fall," said Leon. "Then there's this holiday sing-along on Boxing Day that's a big deal. In between, it can get a little sparse. Unless you're into monster truck shows or the occasional professional wrestling match."

A few people waved at Leon while we were standing in the middle of the street. Leon waved back. "This town is big on waving," he said. "You better get used to it."

An older man in checked golf pants called out in a booming voice, "Hey, Leon. What's new?"

Even though we were only a couple of feet away, Leon raised his voice as he backed away from the man. "Not much, Mr. McHugh." I think he was hoping Mr. McHugh would keep on going. Instead, he headed straight for us.

"Who's your little friend?" Mr. McHugh said, chuckling like this was a joke all three of us could appreciate.

"This is Henry Holloway," said Leon. "He's going to be staying with the Wingates for a while."

Mr. McHugh's smile faded a bit. "Oh, yes," he said. "I think I heard something about that."

"Mr. McHugh won the prize for the biggest squash at last year's Pumpkin Fest," Leon said to me. And then he added, "Henry here is very interested in competitive gardening, aren't you, Henry?"

Mr. McHugh perked up. "Is that so?"

"Not really," I said. Leon looked at me, all disappointed, until Mr. McHugh leaned forward and said, "Speak up, Hank. I can't hear worth spit."

I spoke up. "I'm very interested in vegetable-growing contests."

Mr. McHugh grinned. "Well, stop by the house sometime. I'll give you a few pointers." We shook hands. "Good luck, son," he said. "Watch out for that littlest Wingate. He's hell on wheels."

As soon as Mr. McHugh's checked golf pants were out of sight, I said, "How come you told him I was interested in growing vegetables? I couldn't care less about a festival for pumpkins."

"You say that now," replied Leon. "But in a few months you'll be judging zucchini bread and carving jack-o'-lanterns out of sheer boredom. Believe me, I'm just saving you time."

As we began walking down the street, a woman with a blue tinge to her gray hair stopped to chat. She looked at Leon and said, "Aren't you going to introduce us?" When Leon did, she said to me, "It's always a pleasure to meet one of Leon's special projects. Call me Sylvia, young man." And then, turning to Leon, she asked, "Have you told Henry about Pumpkin Fest?"

"Yes, ma'am," said Leon. "He's very excited about it."

"Where's he staying?" asked Sylvia, like I wasn't standing right in front of her.

"With the Wingates," said Leon.

"Oh, my," said Sylvia. She looked at me sympathetically and said, "I live just a few doors down the street. Drop by any time you feel hungry. I don't care what he's done, Leon. They wouldn't serve Theodora's pot roast in a maximum-security prison."

When Sylvia left, I asked, "What was that about?"

"Mrs. Wingate's very nice. But she's probably the worst cook in Snowflake Falls."

I told Leon that the main drag was beginning to seriously depress me. "Well, I guess we should get to your new home then," he said. "I just wanted to give you a few moments of peace before you meet Oscar."

It was only a short drive to the Wingate's house. Leon said Mrs. Wingate was expecting us, and we walked right into the kitchen after a polite knock on the back door. Mrs. Wingate was scrubbing crayon scribbles off the wall. She was wearing the kind of black horn-rimmed glasses that you see on rocket scientists in really old movies and trying to keep her hair from falling over her fogged-up lenses.

When she noticed us standing there, she stopped scrubbing for a minute. "Leon!" she whispered. It wasn't like your usual whisper. It was a whisper full of relief, like Leon Tully was a Red Cross worker delivering supplies after a natural disaster.

Leon squinted at the crayon scribbles on the wall. "Oscar is very artistic," he observed. "Notice how what he has drawn looks a bit like a lopsided tornado?"

"Not so loud," said Mrs. Wingate, whose expression was practically the dictionary definition of *harried*. "I just put him down for a nap."

"Maybe we can show Henry his room?" suggested Leon.

Mrs. Wingate put down her sponge and gave me a sympathetic look. "Well, Oscar's sleeping in there right now," she said. "And once he wakes up..."

Mrs. Wingate didn't finish the sentence.

"But Henry's supposed to get your spare room," said Leon, squinting at Mrs. Wingate as if he had just caught her cheating at poker. "I know you have one."

"They didn't tell you about the renovations?" asked Mrs. Wingate. She let out a long breath that sounded like a balloon with a slow leak. "The spare room's being expanded. And we're adding a bathroom." She brushed a stray lock of hair off her forehead, but it fell right back to its original place. "We really need another bathroom," she added wistfully.

"Let me get this straight," I said. "I have to share my room with a three-year-old?"

"Actually, Oscar has to share his room with you," Mrs. Wingate said. "And he's still a couple of months away from turning three. I think he's being very generous for his age."

"But what about my privacy?"

Mrs. Wingate got a far-off look in her eye. "Privacy?" she asked, as if she was crawling across the desert, trying to remember what water tasted like. And then she giggled. "What's that?"

I could feel myself turning pale. I looked at Leon and said, "I want to launch an official complaint."

Mrs. Wingate gave me the most pleading look I'd seen since the last time my mother begged me not to steal. It softened me up quite a bit.

"No offense," I said, "but I don't think this arrangement is going to work out." When she didn't say anything, I added, "How much do you know about me anyway? I mean, maybe I'm not a good fit..."

Leon said, "She knows that you—"

"Take things?" said Mrs. Wingate. That's when I really softened up. I guess it was the way she said those two words. Gently. Like I was some forgetful old aunt who kept stuffing things into the pockets of her apron without realizing it.

"I've stolen a car," I confessed, thinking this might be a way out of staying with the Wingates. "More than once."

"What kind?" asked Mrs. Wingate. "I mean what kind was your favorite?"

"I'd have to say the 1957 Thunderbird convertible," I replied, not quite able to keep the pride out of my voice.

"A convertible!" she exclaimed, almost as if she wanted me to go out and steal one on the spot. "I haven't ridden in a convertible in ages."

"Oh, man!" said Leon, who was probably wondering if he should include Mrs. Wingate's thoughts on stolen convertibles in his official report.

Mrs. Wingate must have realized how she sounded, because all the fun suddenly went out of her eyes and they were back to pleading with me. "Couldn't you just try sharing a room?" she asked. "Oscar's really a good boy. He just takes a while to warm up to strangers."

"I already told Henry he was a screamer," said Leon, as if he'd taken care of all the important explaining.

"Does he really bite?" I asked.

"Oscar, bite?" said Mrs. Wingate, laughing a little too hard. "Don't be ridiculous." But her eyes were really pleading now.

My eye caught an upholstered kitchen chair patched with gray duct tape. Just above it, a corner of wallpaper was coming loose. "I guess I could try it for a couple of days," I said reluctantly.

Mrs. Wingate offered me her hand to shake and said, "Call me Theodora." Just then, we were interrupted by the most nerve-racking scream I've ever heard outside of a late-night horror movie. "Excuse me," said Theodora, as if she'd just heard the doorbell.

When she left, I asked Leon, "Is he always this loud?"

"Are you kidding? He's practically on scream cruise control. That's just his casual 'I want out of my crib' scream."

"I don't know much about kids," I said, "but isn't he getting a little old for a crib?"

"I think the bars on the side give everyone a false sense of security," said Leon.

Theodora came back with Oscar in her arms. To look at him, you'd never think it was in his nature to scream or bite. He was still sleepy; his cheeks were flushed and his blond hair was sticking out in all directions, making him look like he'd just stuck one of his little fingers in a light socket. His eyes were big and blue. He had the type of face that looked like it should be on a TV commercial for whatever toddlers ate for breakfast.

Theodora addressed the youngest Wingate very formally. "Oscar," she said. "You already know Leon." Oscar looked at Leon and let out a big belch as if it were his way of saying hello. This surprised everyone, including Oscar, who giggled.

"Oscar," she said. "This is Henry."

I was preparing myself for another volcanic burp, but instead, the kid gave me a big smile and said, "Hen-wee!"

This surprised Mrs. Wingate and Leon even more than the unexpected belch. When I looked puzzled, Theodora explained. "Oscar doesn't talk much." Then her look of surprise gave way to another kind of expression. As if she'd just made an important discovery that was going to brighten her entire day.

"Would you mind holding Oscar for a minute?" she asked me.

"Actually, I would mind very much," I said as politely as I could.

"Just until I finish scrubbing the wall," she pleaded. Next thing I knew, Oscar had been dumped into my arms.

The kid just threw his arms around me and put his head on my shoulder. Before I knew it, his eyes were closed and his mouth was hanging open, leaving a little string of drool on the front of my shirt. I could feel his breath going in and out below my ear. It smelled like overcooked asparagus.

Within a few seconds, Oscar felt like a drooling economy-sized sack of flour. This gave me a queasy sensation in the pit of my stomach. I think Leon sensed my discomfort and decided that it was a good time for him to get out of town. He gave me his business card like he really didn't want me to use it, and Theodora suggested we take Oscar outside so he could snore in the fresh air.

Leon and I stood out on the front porch, watching nothing in particular while Oscar made the sort of noises that should never come out of an innocent baby. A few very slow seconds passed. "Maybe it won't be so bad," I said, doing my best to ignore what my stomach was trying to tell me.

Leon looked doubtful. "Wait till you meet Charlotte," he said.

We stood there for a moment and watched a dog yawn while it peed on a rusty fire hydrant. Then the dog looked at us hopefully, like maybe we could give him a lift out of town. "You're planning your escape right now, aren't you?" asked Leon. Keeping in mind that Leon Tully was a government official, I didn't say anything. A few seconds passed before Leon shot me a look of total pity. "Well, good luck with that," he said. It sounded like he really meant it.

EIGHT

After a while, I knew I couldn't put off going into the house any longer. The bad news was that I had nowhere else to go. The good news was that Mrs. Wingate took Oscar back. She was very happy that he was still dozing. "I think he might sleep for a while longer," she said, as if I'd performed some impossible magic trick. "Have you ever heard of those people who whisper to nervous horses and make them calm down?" she inquired. When I nodded, she said, "Well, maybe you're like a Baby Whisperer. Wouldn't that be exciting?"

"I think I'd rather share a room with a horse," I said.

Mrs. Wingate laughed and asked me to come with her while she put Oscar back in his crib. At first, his room seemed like a typical baby's room. It had wallpaper with a pattern of circus animals on it and all sorts of toys on the floor.

There was also a regular single bed that looked almost comfortable enough for someone like me to sleep in. But since the room was quite small, it sat uncomfortably close to Oscar's crib.

It was hard not to notice the crib because, even if you didn't know much about baby furniture, you could tell right away it was different. The bars on the side were much higher than your average crib. When I pointed this out, Theodora said that the crib was custom-made by her husband. "Harrison calls it the supercrib. Once you get to know him, you'll find he has quite a playful sense of humor."

I looked at the smallest Wingate sleeping peacefully in his one-of-a-kind crib. His little mouth was wide open and contentedly sucking in air. He was snoring loudly with a happy expression on his face. "Why does he need a super-crib?" I asked.

Mrs. Wingate smiled lovingly at her son. "That's a perfectly reasonable question when you're watching him sleep," she said, as if she was searching for the most deli-cate way to phrase her explanation. "I'm afraid Oscar can be a bit of night owl. He used to climb out of his regular crib and go looking for things to do."

She didn't say what sort of things Oscar liked to do in the middle of the night, but they probably weren't very restful. "Does he always snore like that?" I asked. Before I could stop myself, I added, "He sounds like one of those little vacuums people keep in the kitchen to suck up spilled milk."

"It is rather loud, isn't it?" said Theodora. "We took him to the pediatrician about it. But the doctor said there was nothing to worry about. It's probably something he'll outgrow sooner or later."

I looked at the single bed again and asked, "Do you think there's any way it could be sooner?"

"It's hard to tell with Oscar," she replied. "He doesn't do a lot of things the regular way."

And then, as if looking for something positive to tell me about Oscar, she added, "He took to his potty training right away. He hardly ever has accidents anymore."

"That's great."

"It is great," said Mrs. Wingate. "I know he's really bright, but even though I keep telling him the words for things, he never repeats them. Our pediatrician says children develop at different rates, but I think Oscar really can talk. He just chooses not to."

You know how sometimes people give themselves a little pep talk so they can try to believe something they're not really sure of in the first place? Well, that's exactly how Mrs. Wingate sounded. For some reason, I wanted to make her feel better so I reminded her that Oscar had said "Henry." Sort of.

Theodora looked so grateful that I got embarrassed. So I decided to change the subject. "This really is where I'm sleeping, isn't it?" I asked.

"I'm afraid so," said Mrs. Wingate.

"Couldn't I just sleep on the couch?"

"Oh, no," said Theodora, as if I had suggested something that would lead to the downfall of Western Civilization. "That would offend Mr. Wingate's sense of order. He always says, 'The living room is for living, not sleeping. That's why it's called the living room.'"

"He doesn't nap on the sofa?"

"Absolutely not," she replied. "Harrison is philosophically opposed to any form of napping. He considers it a waste of valuable time." Then Theodora looked at me as if she could read my mind. "Oh, I'm sure you and Harrison will get along fine," she said. "The rules in this house are clear as mud."

"I'm not all that good at following rules," I confessed.

Theodora gave me a sympathetic smile. "Just don't mention that awful Bargin Barn. My husband is very sensitive about it."

She started to say something else. But then she noticed Oscar's drool on my shirt. "I can get that right out with a little detergent," she said, continuing to stare at the stain. She seemed to be getting a little emotional about it. For a second, it looked like she might even cry.

"It's just a little drool," I said. "I mean, it's not like he threw up on me or anything."

"Can I tell you something just between us?" she asked. Before I could say no, she said, "Oscar's not really what you'd call a people person."

"What do you mean?"

"I mean, he doesn't take to a lot of people. But he really likes you. I can tell." Just then, Oscar let out a particularly loud snort.

"He seems to be a very advanced snorer for his age," I said.

"I've thought of that," said Mrs. Wingate. She opened the drawer of my bedside table to reveal a brand-new package of earplugs. "Don't let Oscar see these," she cautioned. "He likes to take things from drawers and hide them. I'm still looking for my favorite pair of earrings."

You might think that this was enough for me to digest in one day. But a few minutes later, when Mrs. Wingate and I were back in the kitchen, I had the pleasure of meeting Charlotte Wingate. I could see her leaning her bike against the back porch. It was a pink bike, with goofy-looking white, sidewall tires, a pink basket attached to the handlebars and a lot of girly streamers. There was even an old-fashioned bicycle bell next to the handgrip, the kind that every self-respecting kid used to have on their tricycle.

Before leaving her bike on the porch, she introduced it to me like it was a real person. "This is Gwenivere," she said. "My noble steed."

Even at eleven, Charlotte seemed a bit too old to be riding a bike like Gwenivere. But since she was extra short for her age, I guess she had no choice. I noticed that she had the same rocket-scientist glasses as her mother and wore the kind of clothes that made her look like an undersized vice-principal.

Charlotte began to talk very rapidly, barely pausing for breath. She talked about her work as a crossing guard during the school year. She talked about how many library books she planned to read during the summer. She talked about how she was thinking about becoming a total vegetarian. "I don't understand how anybody could eat a rabbit," she said, "but it's considered a great delicacy in France."

When Theodora left the room to answer Oscar's latest scream, Charlotte began eyeing me thoughtfully through her thick glasses. I felt a little like the rabbit she refused to eat. "Are you sure you're a thief?" she asked. "You have a very trustworthy face."

Before I could answer, she said, "I sincerely hope to play a role in your social rehabilitation." Then she stuck out her hand for me to shake. It looked like she was holding a paddle so that you could step into the crosswalk. "I hope we can be friends, Henry," she said. I figured if I shook her hand she might stop talking. But she went right on telling me about the life of Charlotte.

"I enjoy reading the *Wall Street Journal*, collecting minia-ture snowmen and helping the less fortunate," she said. "Every year I go door-to-door soliciting funds for the Empty Stocking Christmas Fund!"

"I'm not really into Christmas," I said.

"You sound just like Harley Howard," said Charlotte.

"Who's Harley Howard?"

"The town Grinch," she said. "Harley Howard is so cranky and sour that he hasn't attended the holiday sing-along since I can't remember when."

"So what?" I said.

Charlotte looked at me like I'd just confessed to some unspeakable horror. "So what! It's only the single longest running holiday tradition in the history of Snowflake Falls. It takes place in the town square every Boxing Day from six PM to after midnight! It's a way to extend the holiday spirit past Christmas. We sing all kinds of songs and roast hotdogs and marshmallows. Almost everybody turns out for it. It's the social event of the entire season."

Charlotte took a big breath to talk some more. "This year we're having a contest for the town slogan. There's going to be a new sign as you come into town and everything. They're going to reveal the new sign and the new slogan at the sing-along. Isn't that exciting? I'm submitting at least a dozen suggestions."

"I think I'll give it a miss," I said.

"You'll change your mind," she said smugly. Then she leaned close enough so that I could smell the ghost of berry-flavored bubble gum on her breath. "Can you keep a secret?" she asked.

"Absolutely not," I said.

Charlotte just kept right on going. "Before the sing-along on Boxing Day, we're raffling off a five-minute shopping spree at Wingate's!" she exclaimed. "We give the winner a big shopping cart and they have five minutes to fill it up with anything they can fit in the cart." When I said nothing, she asked, "Isn't that brilliant? But you mustn't tell anyone at Biggie's Bargin Barn. We're going to be in direct competition with their hideous Holiday Madness Sale."

"I just told you I couldn't keep a secret!" I said. "And you told me the secret anyway. What kind of person does that?"

"How are you supposed to stop being a criminal type if nobody trusts you?" asked Charlotte. "After all, we have to start somewhere, don't we?" Then she leaned even closer and started to blush. "You know, there's always been a part of me that's wondered what it would be like to actually break the law."

"That's hard to believe," I said.

"I know!" she exclaimed, as if we were suddenly kindred spirits or something. "I can hardly believe it myself."

"Speaking as someone on probation, I would rather not comment."

This did not deter Charlotte. "Do you think I might have a dark side?" she asked.

"I don't think anybody who rides a pink bike has a dark side," I said.

"It's just that sometimes I worry I might not be complex enough," she said. "You know, psychologically speaking."

"I don't know much about psychology," I answered.

Charlotte gave me a look that said she had momentarily forgotten I was a person of lower intelligence. "I guess I'm being a bit of a conversational piggy, aren't I?" she said.

"Now that I've shared everything I like, why don't you tell me everything you like?"

"I like to keep to myself," I said. "Plus, I don't like to share things."

Charlotte didn't get the hint. She just kept talking about her many ambitions. She said she had a natural attraction to the business world and her long-term goal was to take over the family store someday. But in the meantime, she wanted to focus on becoming the youngest hairstylist in Snowflake Falls.

When I observed that hairstyling was a strange ambition for an eleven-year-old, Charlotte did not even bat an eye. "I believe that our outer beauty should strive to express the inner beauty we all aspire to," she said.

Personally, I thought this was an odd statement for somebody who dressed like an elementary school administrator. But I let it pass. In any case, Charlotte kept right on talking. "I haven't actually given anyone a complete haircut yet," she admitted, "but I've been practicing on some of my old dolls."

"I guess it makes sense to do your first few haircuts on customers who can't talk back," I said.

"I'm looking forward to working on someone with authentic human hair. Yvonne at The Cut and Curl thinks I have tremendous potential. By next summer, I might not even have to stand on a box. Here's hoping!" Then she looked at me rather dreamily. "Do you believe in the concept of soul mates, Henry?"

"No way," I said, wishing Mrs. Wingate would come back. "How did we get from haircuts to soul mates?"

"Because I think that maybe I'll meet my soul mate while cutting his hair one day," said Charlotte. "Wouldn't that be romantic?" Her glasses slid down her nose, but she was so carried away that she didn't even bother to push them up. "I believe everyone has a right to true love. Except for maybe those horrid people at Biggie's Bargin Barn."

Just then, Theodora came back into the room. "I see you've met Charlotte," she said to me. "It may interest you to know that she was head crossing guard on the school safety patrol last year." Turning to her daughter, she added, "Maybe you can show Henry the sights tomorrow."

"There are sights?" I asked, imagining Charlotte pointing out all the traffic lights and advising me never to cross on yellow.

"Oh, tons!" said Mrs. Wingate. "And you'll find Charlotte knows just about everything there is to know about local history."

"Oh, Mother," said Charlotte. "Henry doesn't want to hear you brag about me."

While this was certainly true, it definitely sounded as if Charlotte didn't mind hearing her mother brag at all. So Theodora kept right on going. "Charlotte has gotten straight As every year of her academic life," she said proudly. "She's even skipped a couple of grades, and she's about to become the youngest secondary-school student in the history of Snowflake Falls."

Charlotte did her best to look humble. "I'm sure grade eight will be a new and invigorating challenge," she said.

Our conversation was interrupted when Mr. Wingate walked in. He was tall and trim and wearing the exact same glasses as Theodora and Charlotte. Side by side, they looked like they all went to the same closing-out sale on geeky eyewear.

Mr. Wingate had just enough time to introduce himself before we sat down to dinner. I thought he was going to ask me a lot of questions, but he was distracted by the Biggie's Bargin Barn commercial that was playing on the kitchen radio. You could hear the announcer saying, "If we don't give you a friendly howdy as soon as you walk through the door, your next Biggie's purchase is free!"

"Howdy!" said Mr. Wingate hotly, as Theodora turned off the radio with a sigh. "Who actually says that? And the way they leave out the 'a' in *Bargain*!"

"Absolutely no respect for the basic rules of grammar," said Charlotte. "Don't you agree, Henry?"

Oscar, who looked like he was deciding whether or not to throw his spoon against the wall, shouted out, "Hen-wee!"

Mr. Wingate looked at his wife as if his boy had just solved a very difficult algebra equation.

"I know," said Theodora, who seemed eager to change the subject. "That's the second time he's said Henry's name today."

Harrison Wingate looked almost happy. "Way to go, son," he said.

I think maybe Charlotte was a bit jealous. She rolled her eyes and said, "Honestly, you're going to make Henry think that all we do is sit around waiting for Oscar say something."

Mr. Wingate looked at Charlotte sternly and said, "I'm not sure I like your tone, young lady. How would you like me to take away your *Wall Street Journal*?"

"Please, remember our guest," said Mrs. Wingate, who was getting flustered. After that, most of us made an effort to concentrate on dinner. Theodora had laid everything out on the kind of expensive china that I could sell to my old friend Lenny for big bucks. While it all looked edible, I soon discovered that Mrs. Wingate was a truly terrible cook. The lamb chops tasted like an old catcher's mitt, and the peas sat on your fork like pellets from a BB gun.

In spite of this, everybody ate politely. Everybody except Oscar, who was the only one smart enough to keep spitting out his food.

"Look, Oscar," said Mrs. Wingate with cheery desperation. "Henry's eating his dinner all up."

Oscar watched me eating some watery mashed potatoes. "Mmm, good!" I said as if I was auditioning for some stupid TV commercial. You could tell he knew I was lying.

Still, he reluctantly shoved a spoonful of Theodora's mashed potatoes in his mouth. I thought Mrs. Wingate was going to kiss me right at the dinner table.

Later, when it was time to go to bed, Mrs. Wingate decided to have a little conversation with me while checking on Oscar. "You're not at all what I expected," she said, as Oscar snored in the shadowy glow of his clown-shaped night-light. "I mean you're not anything like the others."

"I'm probably worse," I said. "You know what I was thinking when I saw all your beautiful dishes? I was thinking how much I could pawn the whole set for after I stole it."

"Oh, we don't have a whole set," said Theodora, as if her opinion of me hadn't changed in the least. "Oscar's broken at least three of the dessert plates."

"You've got the wrong idea about me," I persisted. "I'd steal your eyeglasses right off your nose if I thought I could get money for them."

Theodora took her glasses off and said, "I don't think you'd get a lot of money for these." She put them on me, and right away I could tell that the thick lenses were nothing more than clear glass.

"I don't get it," I said. "If you don't need glasses, why do you wear them?"

"Because Harrison and Charlotte do," said Theodora. "They have no idea my glasses are fake. Sometimes Charlotte feels rather self-conscious about wearing glasses, even though she's too stubborn to admit it. When we go to the optometrist, she refuses to even try on a different style of glasses though."

"So you wear the same kind even though you don't really need them? Just to make her feel better?"

"I guess you think that's silly, don't you?"

I didn't say anything.

"That's okay, Henry," said Theodora. "If you were a mother you'd understand."

"I won't tell Charlotte," I said. "About the glasses, I mean."

"I know you won't," said Mrs. Wingate. "And Henry? Could I ask you a favor? Just between us? Promise me you won't run away."

Right then would have been a good time to lie. But something about the way Theodora was looking at me made me say, "I can't promise that."

"Maybe we should take it one day at a time," she said. "Could you promise not to run away tonight?" When I agreed, Mrs. Wingate thanked me very sincerely and said goodnight.

I tried to sleep. But everything smelled like baby powder and fuzzy toys. After a while, I noticed Oscar was awake and watching me. "Go back to sleep," I said.

"Seep!" said Oscar, grinning proudly. A couple of minutes later, Oscar was snoring his vacuum-cleaner snore.

I seriously considered reaching for the earplugs in the drawer, but I was afraid the sound might wake him up and he'd spend the rest of the night pestering me.

For a while, I thought about how Mrs. Wingate wore those stupid-looking glasses even though she didn't have too. And then I tried to think of a good reason why Charlotte would insist on wearing the same stupid-looking glasses despite her philosophy on outer beauty, inner beauty and all the kinds of beauty in between. Charlotte Wingate was full of contradictions.

The entire Wingate family was full of contradictions. I got the sense that every one of them wanted to be genuinely normal, but it was just way easier not to fight their natural urge to be seriously loopy. This discovery made it especially difficult to accept my current state of domestic incarceration. All in all, it had been way easier living with the fictional Hendersons.

I curled my pillow around my ears and watched the looming shadow that Oscar's night-light cast on the opposite wall. The bars of the supercrib looked as if they stretched all the way from the ceiling to the floor. "Good night, Uncle Andy," I whispered. And even though I couldn't really hear the words, what with the curled-up pillow and Oscar's snores, it made me feel a little less lonely just to say them out loud.

NINE

I woke up way later than everybody else. Mostly because I'd had the most horrible night's sleep of my life. Oscar was the worst roommate you could ever imagine. When he wasn't snoring, he was awake and saying my name over and over again. "Hen-wee! Hen-wee! Henwee!" When he got tired of repeating my name, he would try out different kinds of screams.

They weren't the kind of terrifying screams that would make Theodora come running. It was more like Oscar was screaming for fun. He'd found the perfect volume for screaming at night. Not loud enough to wake anybody else. But just loud enough to make my life totally miserable.

Finally, I remembered the earplugs. But when I reached inside my drawer to get them, they had vanished. Oscar was standing up in his crib, with his chubby little hands around the bars. "Where did you hide the earplugs?" I asked sternly. He let go of the bars and looked at me, all innocence. Then he shrugged, with his palms up in the air.

"Just go to sleep!" I said.

"Seep!" said Oscar, pointing to his stuffed toy, a little lamb with a missing eye. "Baa-h!"

"Not sheep!" I said. "Sleep!"

But it was too late. Oscar began to run through his collection of barnyard noises. He was imitating the snort of a pig for the forty-eighth time when I realized it had blended into one long snore. I must have managed to sleep for a little while after that, because I do remember opening my eyes in the morning and forgetting where I was.

At first, I expected to see the familiar wooden beams on the inside of Evelyn's tree house roof. Instead, I saw a mobile of circus animals attached to the ceiling. I looked over at Oscar's empty supercrib and suddenly remembered that I was in Snowflake Falls. I pulled the blankets over my face and let out a big groan. Even my worst night in Evelyn's backyard had been better than my first night in Oscar's room.

I thought maybe I would just roll over and go back to sleep for a while, but then I felt a small tug on the bottom of my blanket, followed by a piercing scream. It sounded a bit like a really loud smoke alarm. Except that every once in a while, the smoke alarm would pause for breath before starting right up again.

I looked up from under the covers and there was Oscar, fully dressed and all flushed from screaming. As soon as he saw my face, he broke out into a big smile. "Please don't say 'Hen-wee,'" I begged.

"Hen-wee!" he said, with a high-pitched squeal of glee. Then he opened the bottom drawer of the dresser and started to throw my folded underwear all over the place. "Put down my underwear," I shouted. "And it's not Hen-wee. It's Hen-ree."

After throwing my only clean T-shirt across the room, Oscar squinted at me with his mouth hanging open. Observing his baby squint, I realized that he was probably going to end up needing big clunky eyeglasses. Just like the rest of the Wingates. For a second or two, it made me feel sorry for him. So I thought I'd teach him to make the "R" sound. "Hen-ree!" I repeated. "Hen-ree!"

"Hen-wee!" said Oscar, before racing out of the room and giving me a few moments of valuable peace. When he was gone, I noticed that he had stepped on my only clean T-shirt. There was a perfect outline of his dirty little shoe right on the front.

The next thing I knew, I was staring into the Wingate's bathroom mirror while wearing my stepped-on T-shirt. There were dark circles under my eyes. And no matter how much water I slapped on my face, I still looked and felt exhausted. I was a little slow getting to the kitchen table. Oscar had already finished his breakfast. He was sitting on the kitchen floor, building towers of blocks and then knocking them over. Charlotte was at the kitchen table, drinking vitamin-enriched orange juice and reading the *Wall Street Journal*.

When I asked where Mr. Wingate was, Charlotte told me that he was back from his usual early morning jog, getting ready for another day at the store. When he came downstairs, dressed for work, he looked at his son, busy with his blocks. He crouched down and looked at him very intently. "Oscar!" he said. "What does a sheep say?"

Oscar looked up from his blocks, and Mr. Wingate repeated the question. Since Oscar had made a sheep noise exactly sixty-seven times last night, I was fully expecting the kid to go "Baa-h." But all he did was look at his dad, puzzled. As if he'd just been asked to repair the dishwasher.

Mr. Wingate pulled out a little tape recorder and spoke into it. "Note to self," he said. "Work on the sheep sound with Oscar." He put the tape recorder back in his pocket, looked at Theodora poking at a hardening batch of scrambled eggs and said, "I'll just have orange juice, honey. I'm running a little late."

I was trying to figure out a way to just have orange juice without hurting Theodora's feelings, when Mr. Wingate said, "You know what all great men have in common, Henry? They are early risers."

"I'm not exactly what you'd call a morning person," I said, rubbing my raccoon-like eyes. "I guess I'm just not destined for greatness."

"Why would you say that about yourself, son?" asked Mr. Wingate. "You're admitting defeat before the day even starts."

"Harrison, he was making a joke," said Mrs. Wingate.

"I fail to see the humor, Theodora," he replied. "A family should run like a well-oiled machine. Everybody has to do their part to make sure things go smoothly."

"That's not fair, Dad," said Charlotte. "Oscar probably kept Henry up all night long." Turning to me, she added, "He gets to wreck our well-oiled machine all the time."

Mr. Wingate looked at the dark circles under my eyes. "Is that true, Henry?" he inquired. "Did Oscar disturb your sleep?"

"I guess I'm just not used to sharing a room yet," I said. Oscar knocked down a tower of blocks with a sudden crash that made me jump in my chair.

I suppose Harrison Wingate took a little pity on me, because he said, "Don't worry, young man. We'll have that guest room done before school starts."

"That reminds me," said Mrs. Wingate. "The Nutley brothers phoned to cancel again."

"Again?" said Mr. Wingate, as if he couldn't believe what he was hearing.

"Nutley Construction is doing the remodeling," Charlotte explained. Oscar knocked down another pile of blocks.

"I'm beginning to think it would have been easier just to do the job ourselves," said Theodora.

"You know I can't spare the time from the store," replied Mr. Wingate.

"Maybe we should get somebody else," said Charlotte. "I saw one of the Nutleys buying supplies from Biggie's."

Mr. Wingate looked crushed. "You didn't go in there, did you, Charlotte?"

"Never!" said Charlotte, who explained that she had been looking through the window. "I'd rather die than go inside the Bargin Barn!"

Mr. Wingate gazed at his only daughter with open pride. "I guess we'll just have to find somebody else to do the renovations," he said.

"Harrison," said Mrs. Wingate. "There's nobody else left."

Mr. Wingate considered this gravely. "I'll talk to the Nutleys," he said. Then he pulled out his tape recorder. "Note to self. Talk to a Nutley today." He looked at me and said, "Henry, I've scheduled a private conference with you in the living room this afternoon at three thirty sharp."

While I thought it was unfair to let the living room double as a conference room when not even a single nap was allowed, all I said was, "Yes, sir, Mr. Wingate."

After Mr. Wingate left for work, Charlotte showed me the new bedroom and bathroom that the Nutley brothers were supposed to be working on. The room looked like a bomb had just exploded in it. "This will never be ready in time for the school year," I said to Charlotte. "In fact, I doubt it will be ready for my graduation."

"That was a joke, wasn't it?" asked Charlotte. "I often don't understand what makes other people laugh. One of my goals for entering grade eight is to comprehend more jokes."

But I was more concerned about the state of the spare room than Charlotte's humor problem. "Why is it taking so long to get the renovation done?" I asked.

"My father is meticulous," explained Charlotte. "None of the local tradesmen can tolerate his exacting standards. Especially the Nutleys."

I groaned, and she suggested giving me a tour of Wingate's Department Store to cheer me up.

"Won't your dad be there?" I asked reluctantly.

"He has meetings all over town for most of the day," said Charlotte. "Entrepreneurially speaking, we're in crisis mode right now."

"All because of the new Biggie's?"

"They're taking away a lot of our customers," she said. "We just can't compete with their prices." Charlotte's face began to turn pink with aggravation. "Do you know that there's actually no such person as Biggie?" she asked.

I thought of the huge sign on every Biggie's Bargin Barn: a cartoon figure of Biggie himself, a chubby guy in overalls and a straw hat who snipped away at high prices with a special hedge clipper that looked like a giant pair of garden shears. "They just want you to think that there's some obliging bumpkin cutting prices all day long," continued Charlotte. "Isn't that the most dishonest thing you ever heard in your entire life?"

"I'm not the best guy to ask about honesty," I replied.

"Oh," she said, not unkindly. "For a minute, I totally forgot you're a crook." She began looking me up and down like she was considering returning me to the houseguest store for a full refund. Mrs. Wingate walked into the room just as Charlotte said, "Hmmm…"

"No, Charlotte!" said Theodora.

"Mother, whatever do you mean?" asked Charlotte.

"I mean I've seen that look before," said Mrs. Wingate. "Henry is not your pet. He's a human being."

"But, Mother," protested Charlotte. "Look at those dreadful clothes. He has a footprint on his shirt."

"That was Oscar's fault," I said.

Charlotte rolled her eyes. "Don't use Oscar's behavior as an excuse," she said. "I've never seen anybody in such desperate need of a total makeover."

"Charlotte, you're getting all wound up again," said Mrs. Wingate evenly. "This is just like the time we bought you that rabbit for Easter…"

"Coco has nothing to do with this," Charlotte replied. "Besides, I'm being perfectly reasonable."

"Coco?" I asked. "Who's Coco?"

"Coco Chanel, my rabbit," said Charlotte, who was talking very rapidly. "She ran away. But this is different, Mother." She looked over at Theodora and begged. "Please, can I dress him?"

"Dress me?" I asked, horrified.

"She means pick out some new clothes for you," explained Mrs. Wingate. "The government supplies you with a clothing allowance, and Wingate's would be happy to provide you with your clothes at cost."

"That means we're not making a profit on it," said Charlotte.

"I know what it means," I said. "And I can pick out my own clothes."

"Of course you can, Henry," said Mrs. Wingate. "I was going to suggest you go down there this afternoon—"

"But he has no idea how to dress responsibly," said Charlotte, whose cheeks were getting flushed. "He looks just like the sort of person you might see through the window of Biggie's, hovering over a bin of discount sweatpants." And then, just for good measure, she added, "Henry, if you buy anything at Biggie's, I'll never speak to you again!"

"Promise?" I said, quite sarcastically. "Because, in that case, I will purchase a pair of Biggie's sweatpants immediately."

Charlotte was getting on my nerves. Still, almost right away, I regretted being cranky. Mostly because I could tell by Charlotte's expression that her feelings were hurt. "I'm sorry," I said. "I guess I don't like the idea of taking handouts. From your store or the government."

"You'd rather steal things than accept help?" asked Charlotte. I don't think she said it to be malicious. It was more like she was puzzled and a little curious.

Even so, Mrs. Wingate said, "Charlotte, you apologize this minute."

The next thing I said surprised even me. "She doesn't have to apologize. She's right. I'd rather steal something than take charity any day."

Mrs. Wingate just looked me straight in the eye through her oversized glasses and asked, "So how's that working out for you, Henry?"

I didn't answer right away. First, I thought about how my professional habits had put me on the road that ended in Oscar's snores, Charlotte's bossiness and private meetings in the non-nap room with Mr. Wingate. "Not so good, lately," I admitted.

"Thank you for being so honest," said Theodora.

"Yes, thank you," said Charlotte.

If you are thinking, Boy, that Henry Holloway is turning over a whole new leaf, you would be wrong. In fact, I had already decided that I would liberate myself from Snowflake Falls and the Wingates at the first reasonable opportunity.

Of course, it is always best to be extra cautious when the government has its eye on you. Leon had said he might turn up unannounced "at any time" to check on me. Also, with colder weather approaching, I could not simply return to my former tree house lifestyle. Before taking off, I needed money and a solid plan of action. I had to make sure that nobody would pick up my trail after I was gone.

I figured that maybe the best way to approach the Wingate situation was the same way I approached any strange domicile that I was thinking of burglarizing. Second-rate burglars are perfectly content to find the most convenient way into the place they intend to rob, but the true professional always looks for the most convenient way out before he even thinks about going inside.

I mention this because living with the Wingates was beginning to make me feel a bit like a second-rate burglar. It was as if I had found my way into an unfamiliar house without knowing the safest exit strategy. The only way to determine the best escape route from my immediate predicament was to find out more about the Wingates themselves.

And so, when I said it would be okay for Charlotte to help pick out my new clothes, it was because I wanted to get to know her a little better, if only to find something I could use to my advantage. Something that would help me leave Snowflake Falls behind as soon as possible.

If you think this is a terrible thing to do, you will be happy to know that I was well and truly punished for it. Shopping with Charlotte gave me the worst headache of my entire life. We got to Wingate's, and she made me try on a whole rack of clothes, all the while saying things like, "Notice how this sweater matches your eyes?"

In between wardrobe advice, she began to talk about a dog in the neighborhood named Popcorn. "Popcorn is this little terrier who looks like he should be on the front of a Christmas card," she said. "But he hates strangers. He'll just keep harassing you no matter how fast you pedal."

"Pedal? What are you talking about?"

"I promised I'd let my father explain," said Charlotte. Then she went off to get more shirts.

The one thing I had going for me was that the store was practically deserted. The only person I met was a weird skinny guy who came up to me when Charlotte ran off to see if she could find a pink polo shirt in my size. He was about my age, with a mop of muddy brown hair that stuck out all over the place. His long wrists hung from the sleeves of a cheap red windbreaker that had race-car patches sewn all over it. And his pants were short enough to reveal a pair of sagging, mismatched socks.

"Do I look paler than average?" he asked. "Because I've just donated blood at the blood bank. When the nurse hooks me up, I like to imagine I'm in a war movie, donating rare blood to my best buddy because he's been all critically wounded." He shot me a big grin before adding, "Man, there's so much you can do with a sidekick that you can only pretend to do on your own."

"Do I know you?"

"No, but I know you." He leaned closer. "You're the guy who steals, right?"

I didn't know what to say, so I just nodded.

He stuck out his hand for me to shake so that his long wrist pushed out from his sleeve even farther. "I'm George Dial," he said. "My friends call me Speed."

"Speed Dial?" I said, thinking maybe I heard wrong.

"Cool, huh?" he replied. "It's a nickname I gave to myself. Of course, I don't own an actual vehicle yet. But I am saving up for driving lessons."

"Look, George…" I said, trying to slow down the conversation.

But George Dial did not slow down. "Did you know that Snowflake Falls doesn't even have an actual waterfall?" he asked. "It got its name because of a record-breaking snowfall that took place way back in the olden days. I only mention this because there is many a newcomer who asks, 'Where the heck are the Falls?'"

Then he went on about how cool it would be to go over the Falls in a barrel. If we had a Falls, which we definitely did not. "Nothing exciting ever happens here," he said. "Except for the Monster Truck Extravaganza, of course."

The guy's eyes lit up, and he began to talk lovingly about something called the Devil's Dumpster. He described it as "the world's most totally awesome dump truck." He told me that his gramma's "long-distance boyfriend" was none other than Lloyd "Digger" Finster, who not only owned the Devil's Dumpster but also toured with it all over North America with the Monster Truck Extravaganza.

"Lloyd parks the Devil's Dumpster in my gramma's garage when he visits," said George. "But he never lets me get near the keys because he thinks I would try to drive it." George Dial looked at me gravely and added, "Which I totally would."

Then he did an impression of the Monster Truck Extravaganza announcer. Making his voice go superdeep, he proclaimed, "And now here's Lloyd 'Digger' Finster driving the Devil's Dumpster! So powerful that it could dig a tunnel to the pit of hell!"

After that, he got a tattered magazine clipping about the Devil's Dumpster out of his wallet. It was a huge fire-engine-red truck on gigantic tires with a massive dirt shoveler on the front. There was a trail of bright yellow flame painted on both sides. Lloyd Finster was standing beside the truck wearing a red jacket with yellow flames shooting up the sleeves. "I don't show this to everyone," George said, "but I can tell you're the kind of guy who likes all major forms of transport. Not that I'm psychic or anything," he continued, "but I can see you're staring at my racing patches. Pretty cool, huh? My gramma sewed them on."

George paused briefly for breath before launching into a long speech about how he couldn't decide whether to be a motorcycle daredevil, a stunt pilot for the movies or a rodeo clown who races dirt bikes on the side. "I guess you could say I feel the need for speed!" He broke into an even bigger grin, like I was supposed to know what he was talking about. But I guess he figured out that I didn't.

"Haven't you seen that totally cool movie about the jet pilots?" he asked. "It's about these two guys who are like best friends forever, but in a very cool way. They watch each other's backs and are totally loyal no matter what. That's the way

Speed Dial rolls. That's my personal code. You know what I'm saying? I have the DVD at home and we could—"

I could tell he was going to go on for a while, so I interrupted him. "George," I said, a little too loudly. "How do you know I steal?"

George seemed very happy that all I wanted to do was change the subject. "News travels very fast around here," he said. "And you're the hottest thing to happen in town since our neighbor's basement flooded and nearly drowned their cat." Suddenly he switched gears. "Hey, man," he asked, "has Charlotte told you all that junk about finding her soul mate while butchering his hair?"

When I didn't answer, George plunged ahead. "What a talker!" he exclaimed. "Trust me, after a while everything the Headache Queen says burrows into your brain like a giant power drill."

"The Headache Queen?"

"Charlotte, man," said George. "I'm the one who came up with the nickname, and it stuck. Just you wait. I'm gonna come up with exactly the right nickname for you."

I could feel my own headache getting worse. And Charlotte wasn't even around. "Why would you want to do that?" I asked.

"Because it's what friends do for each other," he replied.

Even though it was starting to hurt my head to speak, I said, "George..."

"Call me Speed, man. All my friends do."

I told him there was no way I could do that. "Why not?" he asked.

"Because I'm not your friend."

"That's cool," said George, like it wasn't really cool at all. "I just wanted to save you from hanging out with the Headache Queen."

"Look, George, I didn't mean to hurt your feelings. I just don't see us being like jet-pilot-type sidekicks or anything."

George started to tug on the sleeves of his jacket, as if he could make them longer. "Save it, man," he said. "You go your way, and I'll go mine."

But before George could go his way, Charlotte came up to me with a fresh batch of pink shirts. "There's one here that's the exact same color as my bike helmet," she said excitedly. Then she noticed George. "Are you going to buy anything?" she asked.

"Hey, I'm a browser," said George. "Browsers have rights."

I asked Charlotte if she had an Aspirin, and George made one last desperate attempt at everlasting friendship.

"You should go to Biggie's for aspirin," he said. "You can buy like a hundred tablets for less than a pack of gum!"

"In case you haven't noticed, Henry and I are in a private consultation about the color pink," said Charlotte.

"No guy should wear pink," said George. "End of story."

Charlotte just glared at him. "I will call Security."

George gave Charlotte a sarcastic little salute. But there wasn't much life in it. It was just to preserve a bit of dignity before he turned and walked away in his mismatched socks. Charlotte's glasses had slid down the bridge of her nose. She pushed them up with her forefinger and said, "You have just met the biggest nerd in Snowflake Falls."

"Is that right?" I said, as I spied my distorted reflection in Charlotte's oversized glasses. I looked like a guy whose head was about to explode.

TEN

When I got to the house for my meeting with Harrison Wingate, I was fifteen minutes late. It was all because Charlotte spent those fifteen minutes making me try on more clothes. Along the way, she got all wound up about the many things she "absolutely adored." She did this at a very fast pace. It was almost as if nobody ever allowed her to speak at home and she was trying to get as much talk in before we hit her doorstep. By the time she started giving me the highlights of her academic career, I was beginning to rethink my plan about getting to know her better.

"Most girls my age think dissecting a cow's eye is gross," she said of her all-time favorite science experiment. "But I found it udderly fascinating." Charlotte paused. For a second, I thought she was just stopping for air. But it turned out that I had annoyed her without even saying a word. "Did you notice I said 'udderly' instead of 'utterly?'" she inquired. "You know, like the udder on a cow?"

"Yes, I noticed," I said.

"So why didn't you laugh?"

"I don't know," I said. "I guess I don't find the parts of a cow all that funny."

"But it has nothing to do with the parts of a cow!" she exclaimed. "It's a pun." She squinted at me from behind her glasses. "You do know what a pun is, don't you, Henry?"

"Yes, I know what a pun is."

"Well, then you know that a pun is a universally accepted form of humor." She continued, "All the books I've consulted say so."

"You read books to try and be funny?" I asked. I couldn't help laughing a little at this. Charlotte looked both puzzled and offended.

"I consult books on virtually all subjects," she said. "As a result, I can fix a flat tire on my bike and do minor plumbing repairs." She stuck out her chin as if she were challenging me to make a big deal out of it. "I have read several different texts on cutting hair," she added. "All I need is someone else to practice on."

I was about to answer her as calmly as possible when she started staring at my face. "Are you drinking enough water, Henry?" she asked. "Because your skin tone suggests that you are not properly hydrated."

"I don't know," I said, trying to ignore the fact that Charlotte was paying attention to my skin. "I only drink water when I'm thirsty."

"But don't you see?" said Charlotte. "By the time you're thirsty, it's too late! The dehydration process has already started!" She gave a sigh that sounded way too big for her size. "I suppose I'll just have to monitor your fluid intake," she said, sounding like some very short nurse on a medical TV show.

"You're going to watch me to see how much I drink?"

"Oh, it's no problem," explained Charlotte. "I always drink more than enough water. We just have to make sure we drink our water at the same time."

"You want us to drink water together?"

Charlotte blushed slightly. "Don't think of it as a commitment to me," she said. "Think of it as a commitment to good health."

"Why don't you drink water with George Dial?" I asked. "He's very pale, and he likes to talk at least as much as you do. You could have a contest to see who would run out of breath first."

"George is a lost cause," said Charlotte. "But there's still some hope for you." Then she began to talk about the stock market, whale migration and the beauty of the Dewey Decimal System. I was a nervous wreck by the time I got to my meeting with Harrison Wingate.

I could tell Mr. Wingate wasn't too pleased to see me. "Henry," he said, "I am very disappointed at your tardiness."

I did my best to explain that trying on a hundred different shirts while Charlotte provided color commentary was very time consuming, but Mr. Wingate went into this long speech about how my behavior cried out for discipline.

I didn't argue, mostly because I knew Mr. Wingate had read Judge Barnaby's full report on everything leading up to my current incarceration in Snowflake Falls. "I can see that Judge Barnaby was right," sighed Mr. Wingate. "You are going to be our toughest case yet." Then he got out a bunch of papers. "I thought maybe your work schedule was a little ambitious. But a little extra work may be just what you need."

"Work schedule?" I asked nervously. "But it's still summer!"

"Surely the judge discussed this with you," said Mr. Wingate, as if I was trying to get away with something. "Your program includes regular employment in the form of part-time work." Mr. Wingate handed me a sheet of paper. "I've taken the liberty of drawing up your schedule."

I looked at the sheet of paper. "It says here that I have to get up at five thirty in the morning!"

"That's correct," said. Mr. Wingate. "Starting next week, you'll have your own paper route."

"A paper route!" I exclaimed. "I'm fifteen years old—not ten!"

"Why, I had a paper route when I was fifteen," said Mr. Wingate, sounding deeply offended. "In fact, I had the very same one."

"But I don't even have a bike," I pointed out. "You can't have a paper route without a bike."

"Charlotte has generously offered to lend you hers," explained Mr. Wingate, as if Gwenivere was not actually a total insult to the concept of transportation.

"But even Charlotte's too old to ride that bike!" I protested. "Plus, she's a girl."

I tried to imagine myself pedaling a pink bike with white-wall tires and pink streamers on the handlebars. But it was just too much for a guy who has driven a 1957 Thunderbird convertible to accept. "Do you not realize that you are asking me to get up at five thirty in the morning to ride a girl's bike down public streets?"

Mr. Wingate pointed out that using his daughter's bike was the only immediate practical solution. "I realize that using Charlotte's bike may spark some undue embarrassment from your less enlightened peers," he said. "Think of it as a valuable exercise in character building."

When I asked Mr. Wingate if he would ever choose to build up his character by riding a girl's bike, he replied, "You are, of course, perfectly free to save for a more masculine bicycle."

"I can't afford a decent bike on a paperboy's salary," I said.

"You will also be working the afternoon shift at Top Kow Burgers," said Mr. Wingate.

"You want me to ride a girl's bike and be a kitchen slave in some junk-food factory?" I asked, not believing my ears.

The more irritated I got, the calmer Mr. Wingate's voice became. "I am merely pointing out that you will be financially compensated for your job at Top Kow Burgers as well," he said. "While it's not a great deal of remuneration, prudent saving will take you further than you might think."

It was just like listening to Charlotte talk, if Charlotte were an older man trying to ruin my life. I looked at the schedule again and noticed that I had hardly any free time at all. "What's all this about Harley Howard?" I asked. "I hear he's a very cranky man."

"Mr. Howard is a distinguished member of the Snowflake Falls business community," said Harrison Wingate. "Unfortunately, he is losing his sight."

"I'm sorry," I said. "But what's that got to do with me?"

"He has requested a volunteer reader. I took the liberty of offering your services, and Mr. Howard has kindly accepted."

"I'm not even going to be paid?"

"Volunteer work is a vital part of your stay here," he said.

"Doesn't the word *volunteer* mean that you agree to do something of your own free will?" I asked.

"Normally, yes." Mr. Wingate nodded.

"Okay," I said, like we were finally getting somewhere. "That means I can't actually volunteer for something I don't want to do."

"We all have to do things we don't want to do, Henry. It's part of life."

"When's the last time you had to do something you really didn't want to do?" I asked.

Mr. Wingate sighed. It looked like he was about to say something. Then he changed his mind and settled for, "We're not discussing me, Henry."

"But what about school?" I asked, trying to keep the desperation out of my voice. "That's starting soon. How am I going to find time to do my homework?"

Harrison Wingate almost smiled at this. "If you refer to your schedule, you'll see that I've budgeted more than adequate time, given your apparently exceptional IQ," he explained. "In addition, you will be required to report to a special school liaison when you start attending Snowflake Falls Secondary."

Mr. Wingate shuffled a few papers around. "Your supervisor at the school will be Ms. Penelope Pendergast," he said. "Ms. Pendergast is a school counselor as well as head of the Home Economics Department. I'm sure she can find some way for you to help out around the school."

I put my head in my hands and said, "This is all way too much!"

Mr. Wingate responded with, "Do you feel we're being unfair?"

When I told him yes through my fingers, Harrison Wingate gave my reply some thought. "Why do you think you're here, Henry?"

"Because I got caught baking cookies in Ambrose Worton's kitchen."

"I mean, what is the purpose of you being here?"

"Punishment?"

"I suppose that's true, from one perspective," said Mr. Wingate. "But that's not the perspective I was talking about." For the first time, I could see a truly kind expression on the face of Mr. Harrison Wingate. "You're here because Judge Barnaby sees something valuable. Something worth cultivating despite your mistakes in judgment."

I said nothing. Mr. Wingate took this as a sign to continue. "So how do we do that, Henry? How do we cultivate your worthwhile side?"

"I don't know," I said honestly. "How?"

"Well, you already know enough about taking, don't you?" he asked. "After all, it's what you do." He paused before adding, "The thing is, you're not so good at giving, are you, Henry? That's what we're here to teach you: how to start giving."

"What do you want me to do?" I asked.

"Ride Charlotte's bike without complaint, for a start. Did you know that Charlotte has taken quite a shine to you?"

"She's not going to try and cut my hair, is she?"

"That was an isolated incident," said Mr. Wingate. "As punishment, Charlotte was forbidden to read the *Wall Street Journal* for an entire week."

I tried to imagine being liked by someone whose idea of a fun time was reading a newspaper that was all about business. I could hear the fear in my voice as I asked, "Did she actually tell you she likes me?"

"She didn't have to," said Mr. Wingate. "She's lending you Gwenivere. It probably seems silly to you, but she loves that bike."

"What kind of person names their bicycle?" I asked. "Besides, you know what she said to me the other day? She said she didn't need any friends. She said all the friends she needed were sitting on the shelves at the library."

"I wouldn't take some of the things Charlotte says too seriously, Henry. Everybody wants to be liked, whether they admit it or not."

The next thing I said just popped out without my thinking about it. "Do you want to be liked?" I asked.

It was a very personal question. But Mr. Wingate chose to answer it very sincerely. "In grade eight, I wanted to be liked more than anything," he said.

I guess I could tell he really meant it. Because I just had to ask, "Did anybody do it? Like you, I mean?"

I could see Mr. Wingate think for a minute. "No," he said. "I honestly don't think anybody did. But Charlotte has something I didn't have at her age."

"What's that?" I asked.

"You, Henry," he said. "She has you. All I'm asking is that you try your best to be kind to Charlotte."

"But why does it have to be me?" I asked.

"Because I believe you know what it's like to be lonely. Don't you, Henry?"

I was watching him get a little anxious as he waited for me to say something back. For a second, it wasn't hard to imagine what he looked like as the kid nobody liked in grade eight.

"Just promise me one thing," I said. "Don't let her come near me with a pair of scissors."

ELEVEN

As far as I'm concerned, the best thing about being a career criminal is that you get to sleep in. Besides my Uncle Andy and his associates, this was probably the thing I missed most about my tree-house life. Now, with Oscar as my roommate, I was beginning to wonder if I'd ever really sleep again, let alone sleep in.

It didn't take me long to discover that there were really two Oscars. There was the daytime Oscar, who spent most of his time coloring on the walls, banging on pots and pans, or throwing my underwear all over the place. He also liked to hang on to the bottom of my right leg until I had to drag him across the kitchen floor just to get myself a drink of water.

Theodora spent most of her free time scrubbing Oscar's artwork off the walls. One day, she pointed to something she was scrubbing off the hallway wall and asked, "Doesn't that look a little like Oscar holding on to your ankle?" To me, it looked like a meaningless scribble. But, knowing how mothers are about their kids, I pretended to agree with her. This made Theodora very happy.

The only good thing about the daytime Oscar? He was so busy wreaking havoc that he hardly talked at all. It was the nighttime Oscar who wouldn't shut up.

The nighttime Oscar liked to keep me up half the night practicing all the words he refused to say in the daytime. During the day, Theodora would point to something like the kitchen stove and say, "Stove." Of course, the daytime Oscar would get that dumb, squinty look and say nothing. But as soon as the lights were out, the nighttime Oscar would keep repeating all sorts of words that came close to regular English. I became an unwilling expert on what I like to call Oscar-speak. He would shout words like "stofe," "fwidge" and "nana" over and over until it just about drove me crazy.

It was almost like he was trying to impress me with his astounding nocturnal word power. Every time I whispered, "Shut up, Oscar!" he would just laugh. Then he would politely adjust his scream to the type of ear-piercing squeal that nobody could hear but me and maybe a few neighborhood dogs.

In between, it was a constant stream of Oscar-speak. "Ca-Pooter!" Or maybe "Lectwisity! Lectwisity! Lectwisity!" Sometimes I would manage to doze off for a minute or two only to be woken up by Oscar shouting things in his sleep between snores. Often they would be his favorite nighttime words all strung together. ("Ca-pooter-lectwisity-nana!") No matter how much I tried to prepare for this, it startled me every time.

I could have requested another set of earplugs from Theodora, but there was no way I was going to let some screechy little kid get the better of me. So I decided to try and tough it out. Unfortunately, this attitude did not do that much for my overall mental alertness.

At five thirty in the morning, the radio alarm clock would go off and the Biggie's jingle ("I like Biggie's! I like Biggie's! We're the best because we're big!") forced me out of bed in the dark—all groggy and sleep-deprived—to fulfill my sentence of delivering newspapers to the eager readers of Snowflake Falls. Oscar would be staring at me, no matter how early I managed to get up and stumble around. Fresh from a few hours of serial snoring, he would shoot me an early morning grin and run through his collection of barnyard noises.

I got so desperate that I even made Oscar "a Lenny sandwich special," consisting of sardines, raw onion and peanut butter on pumpernickel bread. I figured that either he'd hate it and be all mad at me or—at the very least—it might keep his mouth pasted shut until he actually fell asleep.

Do you know what? He loved it. I mean, he ate the Lenny special like there was no tomorrow, gumming his way through it while looking up at me with this weird, almost adoring, smile. Theodora was so grateful to me for making Oscar actually chew and swallow that she started baking completely inedible pies and cakes as my "special reward."

Not only did I go to bed with an upset stomach, but Oscar repeatedly tortured me with a whole new word, which he stretched out like it was the most delicious word in his entire vocabulary. "Saa-mm-ich!"

After a few nights of sharing a room with Oscar, I began to get a little wonky from lack of sleep. It is a scientific fact that sleep deprivation can cause you to imagine all sorts of strange things. I think I was beginning to get what you might call paranoid.

Remember how Judge Barnaby said that people would be watching me to make sure I obeyed the law? Well, I began to notice that various citizens of Snowflake Falls were actually taking notes on me as I went about my business. It got to be that I couldn't scratch my nose without somebody writing it down. Do you have any idea what it's like to be watched all the time? The other day, I was in the grocery store and picked up an apple to check for bruises. Right away, some individual I didn't even know said, "You're going to pay for that, right?"

A few minutes later, I saw a lady look at me and then write something down on a pad. When I accused her of writing a secret report on my behavior, she looked startled and said she was just reminding herself to buy broccoli.

I felt so bad that I went straight to the produce section and got her the nicest-looking bunch of broccoli I could find.

I started to think that everything was a secret test of my probationary conduct. I was in Wingate's Department Store when I noticed that twenty dollars had dropped out of a woman's purse while she was paying for something at the cash register. You have to understand that this is money that had dropped on the floor. To a thief, floor money practically falls into the category of winning the lottery.

The woman didn't notice her lost money at all. It would have been the easiest thing in the world to put my foot over the bill, pretend that I was bending over to tie my shoelace and then pocket the money. But I was so messed up that I just gave her the twenty dollars back. She rewarded me with a very pleasant smile.

I said, "You're going to write this down, aren't you?"

"Write what down?" she asked, totally puzzled. Making me realize that my honest act was completely wasted.

You see what I mean about lack of sleep? It was beginning to make even the simplest tasks seem difficult. For instance, prior to rooming with Oscar, I had absolutely no trouble riding a bicycle. Now, I had to concentrate on pedaling as if I was operating a crane or a small biplane. Even so, I could never get the hang of riding Charlotte's totally humiliating bike. It turned out that the side streets of Snowflake Falls were full of lumps, cracks and potholes. To make matters worse, the noble Gwenivere was too small for me to comfortably maneuver. No matter how hard I tried, I kept knocking my knees against the handlebars.

I was forced to pedal Gwenivere while wearing a heavy bag of newspapers on either shoulder. The two bags were so heavy that they made me swerve all over the road. One bag was for the *Vancouver Chronicle*, which was shipped to town by ferry. This was the "big city" daily that many Snowflakers subscribed to for all their worldly news. The other bag contained a bunch of advertising flyers as well as a weekly local paper called the *Flurry*. It featured such thrilling headlines as "Why Are There So Many Cracks in Our Sidewalks?"

But this was nothing compared to the fact that Charlotte made me wear her adjustable pink bicycle helmet whenever I was riding Gwenivere. The helmet had a whole bunch of stickers on it. But not enough to hide the fact that it was pink. There was a yellow glow-in-the-dark sticker on the side in the shape of a stop sign that read *Safety First!* There was a whale-shaped sticker that read *Save the Whales*. And there was a sticker in the shape of a teddy bear that read *Have you had your special hug today?*

When I protested, she pointed out that helmets were "legally mandatory" in Snowflake Falls. I tried to tell her that, even adjusted to its maximum size, her helmet still felt way too tight for my head. I also made an effort to explain that she was putting me in a very embarrassing situation. Of course, Charlotte wanted to know what was so embarrassing.

"Oh, nothing at all," I replied. "It is perfectly dignified for a fifteen-year-old guy to wear a pink helmet while riding around on a bike that looks like it belongs in Malibu Barbie's garage."

But Charlotte never paid any attention to my sarcastic remarks. It was like I was her responsibility or something. For instance, she would actually get up out of a nice warm bed to observe me put on her safety helmet before I rode off into the savage world of morning newspaper delivery. She'd watch me like a hawk until I swerved out of sight, looking like a pink highlighter pen on wheels. The last thing I saw before pedaling off was Charlotte happily waving at me in a fuzzy bathrobe that had a pattern of leaping bunnies all over it. "Bye, Henry!" she would shout, loud enough to be heard through the double-glazed glass of the living-room window. "Don't forget to watch out for Popcorn!"

As my head throbbed in the semi-darkness, I would marvel at Charlotte's mysterious powers. How—even when I happened to be traveling away from her sincere smile as fast as my knees could hit the handlebars—she could still manage to give me a long-distance headache. You might think, what's the big deal? As soon as the frantically waving Charlotte Wingate is out of sight, all Henry has to do is remove the helmet and toss it in Gwenivere's handy pink basket.

Most mornings, this is exactly what I did. But there were a few times when I was so busy avoiding potholes or trying not to throw papers into a ditch that I actually forgot I had Charlotte's helmet on.

At first, I found pedaling Charlotte's bike down the empty streets to be a very lonely experience. In between banging up my knees and slipping my too-big feet off the pedals, I kept looking out for the little dog named Popcorn, who never showed up. It gave me plenty of time to think of how much I missed Uncle Andy and all his associates. I still carried the Holloway hotline cell phone with me wherever I went, but no matter how much I stared at it, it never rang. Not even once.

To cheer myself up, I began playing a little game. Every morning I looked at a different house on my route and tried to figure out the perfect way to break in. Before long, I knew the best way to get into just about every house on my route. I noticed that a few subscribers didn't even bother to lock their doors. Once in a while, I would imagine liberating a few items, putting them in my carrier sack and pedaling away as fast as the cracks in the sidewalk would let me.

It was the weekly collection day that started to change my outlook. A lot of my customers asked me to help out with other things while they were looking for their wallets. Mr. Reynaldo had very bad asthma and needed me to help him look for his misplaced inhaler. Mrs. Lasky was very grateful when I got her cat out of the backyard tree. And I opened the lid on an especially stubborn jar of pickles for Mrs. Halpern.

I discovered that Mrs. Bellosi had trouble sleeping. No matter how early I stopped to deliver at her house, she was always at her picture window with a cup of coffee. She would smile and tip her cup at me, like it was the official start to the rest of the day.

After a while, I noticed that people were beginning to wave when they saw me on the street. A few of them would say things like, "Keep pedaling, Henry." You know, sort of as encouragement. It was something I couldn't help but appreciate, since I was probably the worst paperboy in the entire history of Snowflake Falls.

For some reason, no matter how hard I tried, I could never throw the paper where I wanted it to go. Most of the time, it landed in somebody's front garden instead of the porch.

As a result, I spent a lot of time retrieving papers out of awkward places. Once—when I was wearing shorts—I scratched my knee on Mrs. Bellosi's rose bushes, and she made me come in to get a Band-Aid. She even insisted on making me a cup of hot chocolate. While she was making it, I had to hear all about her insomnia and how much she missed her late husband asking her where stuff was. "You wouldn't think it was possible to miss someone yelling, 'Loretta, where the heck is my checked sports jacket?' But it is."

At first, I wasn't too happy about socializing with my customers. But Mrs. Bellosi told me that I was a much better listener than the last paperboy. "He couldn't wait to get out of here and sneak a cigarette behind the hedge," she said. "You don't smoke, do you, Henry?"

"No, ma'am," I said.

"Good," she said. "Because I hate cigarette butts around my hedge."

"Who doesn't?" I said, trying to sound as supportive as I could.

My cup of hot chocolate was completely empty. So I thought that would be it. But Mrs. Loretta Bellosi wasn't finished. "I just want you to know that I refuse to believe all those ridiculous stories about you being some sort of juvenile delinquent," she said. "I raised three sons. And I think I know a good boy when I see one!"

She said it proudly. Like she understood human nature and nothing was going to sway her mind in the wrong direction. I didn't have the heart to tell her that I could get into one of her side windows in less than thirty seconds.

Did I mention that George Dial's house was on my paper route? Did I also mention that George enjoyed getting up at six in the morning to watch me deliver his grandmother's paper from the front window? He must have really appreciated my amusement value. Because I could actually see him laughing at me every time I made a delivery.

One day I was riding Gwenivere along my paper route, and George came out to personally greet me. "Man," he said, "I thought there was nothing on wheels this side of a baby carriage that I couldn't relate to." He kicked Gwenivere's fat white front tire and then rang her bell about six times before adding, "You do know this is a girl's bike, right?"

"I gotta go, George," I said. But George Dial was not finished with me yet. He squinted at the teddy bear sticker on the side of my head and asked, "You wanna hug?" He put his palms up toward me like a human stop sign and then added, "No way, man. George Dial does not do guy-hugs unless the other guy is dying from a mortally serious war wound."

Suddenly, I realized that I had forgotten to take off Charlotte's bike helmet. This made me go all red in the face—which made George Dial laugh so hard that I could hear him as I pedaled away down the block.

Unfortunately for me, the daily festival of perpetual embarrassment was just beginning. When I started my job, I was the lowest guy on the fast-food chain at Top Kow. The only good news? I remembered to take off Charlotte's helmet.

I arrived through the kitchen entrance. The first thing I saw was a poster of Top Kow—a cartoon cow who was wearing a top hat with a couple of horns sprouting out of the sides. Even though he was supposed to be a cow, he had humanlike hands. He was pointing a forefinger straight out from the poster. Underneath, there was a caption that read *Aim for the Top! Top Kow Wants You! Discover the Exciting Employment Opportunities that await you in the Fast-Food Industry!* Below it, someone had scrawled *You too can be a minimum-wage slave!*

A little farther down the hall, I came to the kitchen where several people were standing around wearing official Top Kow uniforms. The tunic was made to look like the black and white spots on a dairy cow. But this was the height of fashion compared to the official Top Kow Burgers hat. An oversized baseball cap with Styrofoam steer's horns sticking out of either side and a logo that read *Top Kow is Tops!*

It was a while before anybody saw me standing there. I watched a couple of guys horsing around with an apron. One guy was waving the apron around like he was a bullfighter with a cape. And the other guy kept charging the apron in his official Top Kow cap. He snorted and pawed the ground with one foot. Even if he hadn't happened to be wearing Styrofoam horns, it was easy to tell that he was supposed to be the bull.

There were a couple of people standing around watching, including a tall skinny girl who was smoking a cigarette and trying to look like she wasn't enjoying the bullfighting routine as much as she actually was. The only guy who seemed to be making the most out of the exciting opportunities in the fast-food industry was busy cleaning out the built-up fat in the deep fryer. He was wearing long rubber gloves. But since there was a thick coating of grease up to his elbows, they didn't seem to be doing much good.

Then it was like everybody noticed me all at once. The tall skinny girl stubbed out her cigarette and tossed it in the garbage like she'd had way too much practice. The two bullfighting guys stopped their routine in mid-charge. And the kid who was cleaning out the deep fryer started to scrub even harder.

"Relax," said the apron matador. "It's just the newbie."

I introduced myself. The guy who'd been playing the bull told me his name was Lowell. "Sorry you had to see that," he said. "It gets a bit monotonous around here."

The matador said his name was Stuart. "This is a great place to lose your last shred of self-respect," he explained, putting down the apron.

"Not to mention a few extra brain cells," added the tall smoker. She told me her name was Natalie but that everyone called her Nat. "The little guy up to his armpits in grease? That's Wiley," she said. "Say hello, Wiley."

"Hello," said Wiley. He sounded very depressed.

Lowell laughed. "Hey, Wiley. Where are your manners?"

"Yeah," said Stuart. "Shake the man's hand."

"Very funny," said Wiley.

Everybody stood around for a while debating whether Top Kow was supposed to be a bull or a cow. "He has horns like a bull, but he looks just like a dairy cow," said Lowell, sounding very perplexed. "How can something that's basically a genetic mutant sell so many hamburgers?"

"He's a cartoon," said Stuart. "Cartoons don't have to be anatomically correct."

"There's a limit," added Nat. "I mean, when's the last time you saw a mutant cow in a top hat? What is he, a four-legged tap dancer?"

Just then a small speaker that stuck out of the wall opposite the stove began to crackle. You could hear a distorted voice going, "Hello? Hello? I'd like to place an order."

"Drive-thru alert!" barked Stuart, like he was a big-time submarine commander.

"Battle stations!" shouted Lowell. Everybody but Wiley started to move around very quickly. With their Top Kow caps on, it looked a little bit like a very small stampede. Lowell grabbed a supersized cup of Top Kow orange soda and started to chug-a-lug. Stuart grabbed a supersized cup of Top Kow cola and did the same. Meanwhile, Nat went over to the speaker, pressed a button and spoke. "What can Top Kow Burgers do for you?" she asked very sweetly.

Stuart and Lowell huddled close to the speaker as the distorted voice replied, "I'll have a deluxe TK burger..." Just then Stuart let out the biggest, most stretched-out belch I'd ever heard in my entire life. You could tell it really startled the customer, who inquired, "What the heck was that?"

"What was what, sir?" asked Nat innocently. "Please continue with your order."

"Let's see. Umm…That was a deluxe TK burger and large fries and…" Lowell let out his own gigantic belch. It was even more impressive than Stuart's. In fact, I couldn't hear anything else until the distorted voice declared, "I know I heard something that time!"

"What was that, sir?" asked Natalie, as Stuart and Lowell began to recharge with quick gulps of soda.

The distorted voice began to shout. "I said large fries—"

Just then both Stuart and Lowell let out a massive belch together. From where I was standing, they looked like two opera singers hitting a high note. When it was all over, I could hear the voice on the other end saying, "…don't need this. I'm gonna go home and make myself a salad!" Nat, Lowell and Stuart did a little victory dance and gave each other high fives.

"I'm impressed," I volunteered.

"It's our dream to move to Hollywood and become professional belch artists," explained Lowell.

"When some movie star can't belch on command, we will do the belching sound effect for them," explained Stuart. He looked over at Wiley, still cleaning the fryer, and added, "But we will never forget the little people, will we, Why-me?"

Natalie explained that Wiley got his forlorn nickname because he was Top Kow's longest surviving "Grease Pig"— the worker responsible for the lowest, dirtiest jobs in the kitchen. She looked at him like he was seriously misguided.

"Why-me wants to be Employee of the Month real bad," she teased. "Don't you, Why-me?"

Wiley rolled his eyes toward the ceiling. "Why me?" he asked, which made everybody laugh.

"Spoken like a true Grease Pig," said Lowell, who let go with a final belch to emphasize his point.

"Wiley doesn't like it that we try out our best practical jokes while Rat-boy's on his fresh-air break," said Stuart.

"Who's Rat-boy?" I asked.

"That's what we call our manager," said Nat. "He's a real jerk."

"He calls us all by our last names," said Stuart. "Like we're in the Marines or something."

"Nat's Wosney and Why-me is Brubaker," said Lowell. "I'm Krakowski and Stuart is Warren."

"Rat-boy hates my last name because it sounds like a first name," said Stuart. "He thinks it breaches the chain of command."

"He sounds awful," I said.

"We have ways of getting even," said Nat.

"We've convinced him there's a rat loose around here," explained Stuart. "Just to mess with his head." Stuart said they named their phantom rat Russell. "Rat-boy actually thinks he's seen Russell once or twice. It's driving him crazy."

"He's already called the exterminator three times," said Nat. "Now the guy wouldn't come back even if there was an actual Russell sighting."

Lowell rattled off a whole bunch of his pet peeves about the manager. How he turned the supply closet into his own private office. How he's always trying to be inspirational by saying things like, "Wear the horns with pride!"

Stuart interjected that Rat-boy probably wore his Top Kow cap to bed at night. "Plus, he is drunk with power and rants at us over every little thing," he added. "When he gets going, it's like he gives a whole new meaning to the words *mad cow.*"

"You guys just don't understand the pressures of being an executive," said Wiley.

"Why-me loves Rat-boy," explained Lowell. "He's eternally grateful for the opportunity to specialize in all major forms of scum."

"It's gonna pay off some day," said Wiley. "Wait and see."

That's when Rat-boy walked in from his fresh-air break.

I must say, I was surprised to discover that we'd met before. Just to make sure, I checked out Rat-boy's socks. They were still mismatched. "Hello, George," I said.

George Dial ignored my greeting. Instead, he sniffed the air—which made him look a little like an actual rat—and announced, "Someone's been smoking!" He looked at Nat and sputtered, "Last time was your final warning, Wosney. You leave me with no choice. You're—"

"I was the one smoking," I said. "Wiley tried to tell me it was against the rules. But I just wouldn't listen."

George looked toward Wiley. "Is that true, Brubaker?"

Wiley nodded.

"Okay, Brubaker, you're off fryer duty," said George. "That's Holloway's job until further notice."

"I've been promoted to mop detail?" asked Wiley, as if he couldn't believe his good fortune.

George nodded. "Report to my office in five minutes, Holloway," he said. "I'll assign you a locker and issue you an official uniform."

Then George Dial disappeared behind the door of his private broom closet.

"Do you realize what has happened here?" Stuart asked me. "He just made you the new Grease Pig."

"Why me?" I asked, sounding just like Wiley, who was jumping around shouting, "Free at last!"

Lowell put his arm on my shoulder sympathetically. "When you're in Rat-boy's office, would you mind telling him you saw Russell with a mustard packet in his teeth?" he asked. "That would really freak him out."

"Why not?" I replied. "What have I got to lose?"

Nat smiled at me gratefully. "Welcome to Hamburger Hell," she said.

TWELVE

By the beginning of September, I had spent over a month in Snowflake Falls. That's four whole weeks of Oscar keeping me up all night long and Charlotte pestering me the rest of the time. Even when Charlotte and I weren't together, she would often follow me at a distance on her bike. "Why are you following me around all the time?" I would ask.

"It is my civic duty to see that you don't steal anything," she would reply.

As if Charlotte's superior attitude wasn't enough emotional torture, my time in Hamburger Hell was turning me into a human chew toy. It was Wiley's vast experience as a former Grease Pig that clued me in to why dogs had started chasing me on my paper route. "The smell of grease has a way of sticking to you like bacon-scented aftershave," he explained, advising that I should protect my ankles from bites by wearing several pairs of extra socks. "Trust me," he added. "Big dogs will chase that smell for blocks."

But no dog was worse than Popcorn, who had suddenly decided to make a regular appearance on my route. At first Popcorn was just a white blur attached to a bark that sounded like the world's smallest chainsaw. Most dogs would give up after a couple of blocks, but Popcorn just kept going until he was tired out or managed to get some of his teeth into the outer layer of my sock armor. This could go on for several blocks.

I talked to Popcorn's owner, who was a very nice man named Lyle Kurtz. Mr. Kurtz said that he'd been keeping Popcorn inside the house for weeks because his spirits had been way down lately. "I think he really missed chasing the last paperboy," said Mr. Kurtz. "I've tried different dog treats. But nothing pepped the little guy up until he saw you pedaling down the street."

I asked Mr. Kurtz if he could keep his dog inside until I finished my route. "But you're the highlight of his day," he said. "It's the only way he gets any exercise. I take him for walks, and he flops down in the middle of the sidewalk like a puddle of milk."

When I protested that Popcorn was interfering with my delivery duties, Mr. Kurtz said, "You're not afraid of a little dog, are you?"

"Only because I'm running out of socks."

"He'll stop chasing you as soon as he gets to know you."

"When's that going to be?" I asked.

"It's hard to say," said Mr. Kurtz. "No offense, son. But when the wind shifts, you smell a little like a deep-fried taco."

"It's a long story," I said.

Mr. Kurtz took a ten-dollar bill out of his wallet and stuffed it in the front pocket of my shirt. "Look, just let him chase you for a while. It's good for his morale. Odds are he'll just chew up the hem of your pants. But if he gets lucky, I'll spring for the tetanus shot and a twenty-dollar bonus for pain and suffering."

I was going to tell Mr. Kurtz to forget it, but then he looked at me and said, "Thanks for giving me back my dog, son. It means a lot."

To make matters worse, I was now an official student at Snowflake Falls Secondary. While this gave me a break from Oscar, it also meant that Charlotte knew exactly where to find me at all times. It turned out that the school Charlotte was even worse than the summer-vacation Charlotte. The first thing she said when she saw me in hall? "A gentleman would carry my books."

"I'm no gentleman," I said. But because Charlotte was Charlotte, I ended up carrying her books anyway.

To make matters even extra worse, I was now under the watchful eye of Ms. Penelope Pendergast during school hours. Twice a week, I had to rush through my morning paper route so I could spend forty-five minutes of precious free time being counseled by her. "No offense," I said when we were first introduced, "but I'd rather be sleeping."

Ms. Pendergast thought this was highly amusing. "There's nothing like a good laugh to start the day right," she said. "Don't you agree, Henry?"

At first, I thought Ms. Pendergast was being sarcastic. But this is not the Penelope Pendergast way. Even to the most casual observer, it's clear that she is an optimistic person who believes that everyone is basically good at heart.

Ms. Pendergast was also a knitter; she always had a sweater or scarf in the works. Being a Home Economics teacher, she would often have a fresh-baked blueberry muffin waiting for me. This gave me something to look forward to during our morning conferences.

I don't want to give you the idea that Ms. Pendergast was some sort of elderly lady. She dressed very stylishly and had the kind of haircut that always looked naturally in place and she smelled a little like vanilla extract, which was actually quite pleasant. She was very big on smiling as a form of encouragement. Not that I gave her much to smile about.

During our last meeting, I was buttering the top of my blueberry muffin, when she asked me for an update on my progress in Snowflake Falls. "Well," I said, "I'm the new Grease Pig at Top Kow Burgers."

This made Ms. Pendergast smile with encouragement, until I informed her that being a Grease Pig was not like a promotion at all. "Think of it this way," she said. "You're in the best possible position to rise above it all."

I thought maybe Ms. Pendergast was going to make me write a series of reports on how I was getting along in Snowflake Falls. Instead, she said, "I just want you to get to know everyone, Henry. Your assignment is to introduce yourself to at least one stranger every day. Can you do that for me?"

There was something about Ms. Pendergast that made me not want to disappoint her. So I started going up to strangers and introducing myself. "Hello," I would say. "My name is Henry Holloway and I'm new in town."

I noticed that a few people automatically felt for their wallets before returning my greeting. But for the most part, everyone did their best to be nice. On the other hand, meeting an entirely new person every day can really drain your energy. No matter what their disposition.

Early in September, Leon came back to town to make his report. I filled him in on everything. "You don't look so good, Henry," he said. "I'll make a note of the bags under your eyes."

"I'm stressed-out, Leon."

Leon narrowed his eyes. "I can't say for sure, but I think you're developing a nervous twitch."

I pleaded with him. "I only get a few minutes of sleep a night. And when I do, I have these terrible nightmares about Popcorn. I need to get out of Snowflake Falls."

He nodded but said there was "a slight problem." Judge Barnaby was getting reports from various town spies about how I was finding lost asthma inhalers for people and getting cats out of trees. While Leon told me he was very sympathetic to my predicament, he said Judge Barnaby felt I was showing hopeful signs of becoming a solid citizen.

My only relief was writing letters to Uncle Andy. I wrote him one almost every day. They were long letters all about the people who were driving me crazy in Snowflake Falls. I mailed them all to my uncle's prison with the appropriate postage. But I never got a single reply back.

On top of having to be unnaturally honest and considerate all day long, I had to put up with having Charlotte join me for lunch in the school cafeteria. Needless to say, she did very little eating and a lot of talking. Of course, there were those individuals who considered my embarrassment a highly popular form of lunchtime entertainment. They gathered around in a group just to watch my face turn red while Charlotte took fifteen minutes to explain why she always cut the crusts off her sandwiches.

"That's the way English royalty does it," she would say, before going on and on about some dead king who got his head lopped off like the crust on her lunchtime sandwich.

Sometimes, it was just too much. One day Charlotte looked at me from across the cafeteria table with those stupid rocket-scientist glasses of hers, and I asked, "How come you don't invest in a pair of contact lenses anyway?"

"I can't wear contact lenses," she answered matter-of-factly. "They irritate my eyes."

"So why don't you at least get a cooler pair of glasses?" I inquired.

Charlotte started to get all wound up again. "Because these glasses are just like my dad's," she said. "I'll never take them off, and my mom will never take off hers either. You know why?"

"Why?" I asked, mostly because I knew she was going to tell me anyway.

"Because the Wingates are a team," she said. And then, just in case I didn't get it, she added, "We're Team Wingate!"

Charlotte informed me that—even though I didn't wear glasses—she considered me an official member of Team Wingate. Mostly this meant that she would ask my opinion on everything. Just so she could tell me how wrong I was.

Yesterday she insisted on showing me this book called *Famous Hairstyles Through the Ages*. There was a specific page marked with a red plastic drinking straw. It showed a picture of a Roman soldier with very short hair. "What do you think of this hairstyle, Henry?" asked Charlotte, while eyeing my skull with great interest. "I think it projects a great deal of masculine authority."

"Stop staring at my head like that," I said. "And anyway, why do you want to become a hairstylist so much?"

"Are you serious?" she gasped. "The money a good conversationalist can make in tips is fabulous." Then she looked at me very seriously. "When I become the best hairstylist in town, I'm going to donate all my tips to the Empty Stocking Christmas Fund."

You would think that my job at Top Kow Burgers would be a welcome break from Charlotte. But it didn't take me long to realize that George Dial was doing everything he could to get back at me for not leaping at the golden opportunity to be his DVD-watching best friend.

I scrubbed every surface of the kitchen until my hands were raw and my feet were aching. I took out the garbage and set George's homemade traps for Russell the rat. Even though Russell did not exist, it did not stop me from regularly getting my fingers caught in the spring-activated traps. In addition to which, the crappy garbage bags would regularly split open, leaving me covered in old hamburger wrappers, leftover fries and congealed milkshakes.

After the last split-garbage-bag incident, I visited George in his broom-closet office with the idea that maybe I could get on his good side. I stood there for a while, looking at the many pictures of monster trucks and cars that were pasted to the wall next to all his Employee of the Month award certificates. When he finally looked up from his paperwork, he asked, "What is it, Holloway? I'm busy here."

I explained to George that my Hamburger Hell duties were getting to me. "Come on, Speed," I pleaded. "Give me a break."

George Dial glared at me, like I had made a big mistake. "Only my friends call me Speed," he said. "And you're not my friend, are you, Holloway?"

The guy looked so ticked off that I just had to ask him one last question. "How come you hate me so much, George?"

George thought about his for a moment. "I don't hate you exactly," he said, dropping his super-officious manager's voice and sounding almost human. "I'm just majorly disappointed, you know?"

When I asked him why, he said, "I guess I heard about you and my imagination took over. I thought you were going to be some big-time jewel thief or something." George looked at me, all forlorn. "In case you haven't noticed, nothing exciting ever happens in this town."

"What do you expect me to do about it?"

"I don't know," said George, looking even more forlorn. "I guess I just didn't expect you to be so…ordinary."

It sounded so bad that I felt the need to defend myself. "I never used to be ordinary," I said hopefully. "I used to steal fast cars and go to the opera in the middle of the day and eat French pastry for lunch."

"How does that help me now?" asked George.

"I'm on probation, George," I explained. "Being ordinary is my only choice right now."

"At least you have a good excuse," he said. "I know what everyone out there says about me, you know. You think I like being responsible all the time?"

"Everybody jokes around," I lied. "It's nothing personal."

"You know there's a rat around here somewhere," said George. "I've seen it. At least I think I have. And that's no joke." Then he looked at me sorrowfully and added, "You don't think I'd enjoy doing something totally fun and irresponsible?"

"So why don't you?" I inquired.

"It's no use," he answered. "You just don't understand the burden that comes with entrepreneurial leadership."

At this point, I was frantically trying to think of something that would make George feel better. "Cheer up," I said. "The monster truck rally is coming soon and the Devil's Dumpster will be parked in your gramma's garage."

"Yeah." He sighed. "All I can do is watch somebody else have all the fun."

He sounded so depressed that I finally gave up trying to cheer him up. Cutting to the chase, I asked, "Isn't there anything else I can do to be promoted from Grease Pig?"

Much to my surprise, George replied, "I'll think about it." Then he snapped back into manager mode—telling me to straighten the bill of my cap ("The Top Kow manual states that your horns should be properly aligned at all times.") before doing a surprise inspection of my fingernails.

You might think, How can Henry's life get any worse? But somehow it managed to do just that. At first, I didn't think that being a volunteer reader for Mr. Harley Howard was going to be so bad. I mean, it had to be less stressful than standing up to my armpits in hamburger grease. Then I met Harley Howard. "There's only one thing I respect less than a thief," he said, by way of introduction. "And that's a thief who's stupid enough to get caught."

It turned out that Harley Howard was by far the richest man in Snowflake Falls. Charlotte told me that he was a businessman who had made a lot of money and then retired and had come to live in Snowflake Falls because it was his wife's hometown. Then his wife died and he became the town hermit, wasting away in this big old mansion.

Harley Howard's house was extremely untidy, full of over-flowing ashtrays and layers of dust. But even the dust couldn't hide the value of all his possessions. Everywhere you looked, there was something that would have made my friend Lenny dance for joy. I noticed that he had the most expensive stereo system I'd ever seen. "Touch anything and you're toast," said Harley. "That goes double for my record collection."

"What would I want with a bunch of old records?" I asked.

"They're extremely valuable collector's items," said Harley. "Among other things, I have every recording Frank Sinatra ever made. I don't suppose you know who Frank Sinatra is?"

It so happens that Frank Sinatra was a great singer of the kind of music my mother liked to play on the piano. I know this because my mother liked to talk about how great he was all the time. "I know who he is," I said.

Harley Howard snorted. "So name three songs he liked to sing."

I named four songs and then stopped. Harley Howard looked amazed. "My mother liked him," I said.

"Your mother had good taste," he said. Then he looked at me and didn't say anything for a while. I thought he wasn't going to talk at all until he said, "I had one hell of a singing voice, you know. They used to call me the Frank Sinatra of Snowflake Falls."

"Did you participate in the Christmas sing-along?"

"Participate? I was the Christmas sing-along. But that's ancient history."

"You don't sing anymore?"

"What for?" he said. "There's nobody around to listen. Nobody who matters anyway."

It was hard to imagine Harley Howard singing. Or having any kind of fun at all, for that matter. He had a couple of wisps of gray hair sprouting from the sides of his head. Because he couldn't see very well, he squinted a lot. This made his face resemble an unhappy prune.

Harley Howard's favorite expression was "bullcrap," which he used to punctuate some of his most sincere thoughts. "Losing your sight is one bullcrap of a deal, Holloway," he observed. "I'm just sitting here watching everything fade away. You know the worst part? It's the boredom.

When you're going blind, they say your other senses get stronger," he said. "So you end up hearing like an owl. So what? It's a load of bullcrap." He thought about this for a moment and gave a laugh that sounded like somebody walking through a pile of dry leaves.

It turned out that I was Harley Howard's fifth volunteer reader. Everybody else had quit because Harley was known for miles around as the crankiest man in town. Plus, he lounged around all day in the world's most expensive bathrobe while smoking the worst-smelling cigars on the planet. His library featured a whole bunch of dusty wedding and anniversary photos of Harley Howard and his late wife.

Harley looked very happy in all the pictures. After a while, he noticed that I was looking at them. "That's my wife Vivian," he said. "Everybody in town loved her, and she loved every last dumb hick in this town." He coughed dryly. "I still don't know what the hell she saw in me."

"Maybe she liked the way you sang," I said.

"Don't sass me, kid. If there's one thing I can't stand, it's sass from a juvenile delinquent." I was going to tell him that I didn't mean to be disrespectful when he asked, "Can you read?"

I figured it was best to keep my answers short. So all I said was, "Yes."

My major duty was to read to him from a thirty-volume series of leather-bound books entitled The Universal Library of Immortal Literature. Harley Howard explained that the books had been a gift from Vivian. "Before Vivian passed away,

I made her a solemn promise that I would read every single volume," he said. "Vivian felt that I was basically an overgrown kid with no taste for refinement or culture whatsoever."

Harley Howard blew a perfect smoke ring with his cigar. "She was right, of course," he added. And then, as the smoke ring disappeared wistfully into the air, he said, "She was right about everything."

"I'm sorry she died," I said before I could stop myself.

"Who asked you?" snapped Harley Howard. And then he let out a deep sigh and said, "You know something? I'm not sure I want a thief hanging around my house."

I said, "I guess you think I'm going to rob you blind, huh?"

Maybe you are thinking, Why would Henry say such a stupid thing? Well, for one thing, Harley Howard made me more nervous than anyone in Snowflake Falls—and that is saying a lot.

Of course, I wanted to take the comment back as soon as I said it. But before I could apologize, Harley Howard actually laughed his walking-through-dry-leaves laugh again. "What's that expression supposed to mean anyway?" he asked. "I mean, how can anybody but God have the power to rob a person blind?" He didn't wait for me to answer. "Maybe God's a thief too, eh, kid? That would explain a lot."

Just the way he said it, made me think of my mother. "I guess maybe it would," I agreed.

Maybe Harley could tell I was thinking about someone I missed because his voice got a little softer for a moment. "This town is full of people who want something from me," he confessed. "They all think I sleep with a million dollars stuffed under my mattress."

"Do you?" I asked, unable to keep the sound of hope out of my voice.

"You wish," he said sourly. "Not that I couldn't if I damn well felt like it."

"Really?" I said, getting a little excited at the thought of my number-one burglar fantasy coming true.

I guess Harley Howard thought this was amusing. Because he just about smiled. "Did you notice that stretch limo parked in front of my house?" he asked. "It's the sweetest ride in town. And I park it on the street so everyone can see it's mine." When I asked if he actually drove it, he said, "Don't be ridiculous. Harley Howard doesn't drive. Harley Howard gets driven."

I asked him how rich a guy would have to be to have his own chauffeur. "Let's just say that I've lost more money through the hole in the pocket of my pants than you'll ever see in your lifetime." He snorted. Then he softened up again and asked, "You like money, huh, kid?"

"Just the kind I find lying around," I said.

"What do you know?" he said, his voice filled with surprise. "A teenage thief with a sense of humor." Then he got all serious on me. "Before you get any ideas,

I have an excellent security system," he warned. "Not even your devious little mind could figure it out." He waved his cigar at me and said, "Aren't you even a little curious about the setup?"

"Not in the least," I lied.

"That's a wagonload of bullcrap," he said. "Right this second you're thinking, I wonder if the old guy has sacks and sacks of money lying around the place? I wonder if his hobby is rolling around in piles of loose cash?"

"Maybe I'm a little curious," I confessed.

This made Harley Howard laugh so hard he broke into a hacking cough. "Tell you what, kid," he said. "I'll make you a little wager. If you can break into this house without disturbing anything, I'll owe you a favor."

"What kind of favor?" I asked.

"Any kind you want. And let me tell you something else. In this town, a favor from Harley Howard is money in the bank."

"What's the catch?" I asked.

"If the alarm goes off, you become my personal slave," he replied. "That includes cleaning out everything from the toilets to the ashtrays."

Personally, I was very offended at the thought of cleaning somebody's house in any manner without having burglarized them first. "Don't take this the wrong way," I replied, "but I can see why nobody in this town likes you."

Harley Howard acted as if I had paid him a great compliment. "Make up your mind, kid," he said, blowing another leisurely smoke ring. "Do you want money or do you want people to like you? Because, in my experience, the two things just don't go together."

After that, Harley Howard requested that I read a poem called "The Charge of the Light Brigade." As I started to read, I couldn't help but think that Harley Howard was having a good time picturing me scrubbing his floors.

That night, while listening to my roommate's buzz-saw snores, I kept thinking about what the old man had said to me about making a choice between money and people. I was just about to decide that maybe money was the right choice when I thought I heard the sound of a tiny pebble against the windowpane. When I heard it again, I went to the window and opened it.

Standing down below, were none other than Cookie Collito and Wally Whispers. At first, I thought I was dreaming. But then Wally whispered, "Don't worry, Henry. You are not dreaming." Naturally, I wanted to join them, but Wally said they would talk to me in the morning. While we made arrangements to meet, I asked if they knew their way around town. Cookie told me not to worry. "We'll find you eventually," he said. "Word on the street is that you are riding a very girly bike."

THIRTEEN

In the early hours of the morning, I met Wally and Cookie on my paper route. There was an empty house on my route that was up for sale. First, we made sure nobody was watching us. Then Wally kindly offered to pick the backdoor lock. "Since this is your turf, you should rightly do the honors," he said, shortly before we made ourselves at home in the empty kitchen. "But I do not want you tainted by any criminal activity while you are under government surveillance."

It turned out that Uncle Andy had been sharing my letters with his associates, so both Wally and Cookie were pretty much up to speed on my recent activities. I must say I was very glad to see them both. Naturally, I assumed they had come to take me home.

But Wally pointed out that they were staying at the Friendly Neighbor Motel and would leave town without yours truly as soon as Snowflake Falls wore out its welcome. "I do not have a home to take you to," apologized Wally. "Unless you count my most recent stay as a guest of the penal system."

Having been kicked out of his cranky cousin's apartment, Cookie volunteered that he was also without a permanent address. Cookie said he thought it was a shame that a nice town like Snowflake Falls did not have a golf course big enough to be worthy of his talents. "I fear that I will have to look for temporary employment of an honest nature," he said, looking very downcast.

I asked them why they were hanging around town in the first place. "We are here at the request of your beloved uncle," explained Wally. "Given his current lack of mobility, he wishes to confirm once and for all that you are in the proper domestic environment."

"Also to make doubly sure that you are not actually staying with some make-believe family who bakes invisible bread," added Cookie, sounding very hurt that the Hendersons did not actually exist.

When I apologized very sincerely to Cookie for deceiving him about the Hendersons, he assured me that all was forgiven. He confessed that his return visit to Evelyn's house had been an unexpected surprise, mostly because he encountered Evelyn. "Fortunately, I was able to improvise some story about inspecting the premises for cockroaches," he explained. "Evelyn was deeply concerned. Until I offered my professional opinion that her house was probably not yet infested."

After explaining to Uncle Andy's associates how grateful I was for their concern, I worked very hard to convey the ceaseless agony of my life in Snowflake Falls. "They are making me read as a condition of my parole," I explained. "Plus, a dog named Popcorn keeps mistaking me for a TK deluxe bacon burger while I'm throwing newspapers into the bushes."

Cookie and Wally were sympathetic, but they both felt that my current imprisonment was the best thing for me. "You are getting a roof over your head and three meals a day," said Wally. Having heard my complaints about Mrs. Wingate's cooking, he added, "Three indigestible meals a day, but still…"

"Also, your job as a newspaper thrower supplies you with all sorts of fresh air," added Cookie. With this, Wally observed that I was going to be late for the rest of my paper route. He stressed that, for my own good, I should pretend they were total strangers, ones without lengthy criminal records. "We do not know each other," said Wally. "Even though you can rest assured that this is actually not the case."

Knowing that I wasn't going home with Wally and Cookie made me feel extra melancholy and homesick.

Then something very strange happened. A couple of days after our meeting at the empty house, I saw Wally Whispers walking along the main drag of Snowflake Falls with Mr. McHugh. They were laughing and having a great time. Wally was saying, "No kidding? How many BLT's do you figure you could get out of a tomato that big?" When I caught Wally's eye, he pretended that he didn't even know who I was.

Things got even more interesting when I saw Cookie the following day. I was walking past Biggie's, and there he was—wearing the bright orange smock of an official Biggie's greeter. Naturally, I went inside to see what he was up to.

Cookie had on a big name tag that said *Hi! My name is Donny!* I watched him talking to a bunch of people like they were old friends. Mrs. Halpern came up to him, and he said, "Gloria, how's that new clock radio working out?" Then he said something I couldn't hear, which made Mrs. Halpern exclaim, "Oh, Donny! You're such a kidder!"

I was so shocked that I forgot to pretend not to know who Cookie was. When I tried to talk to him, all he said was, "Howdy, stranger! Make sure you don't get permanently injured by the avalanche of bargains here at Biggie's!" Then—never one to resist a free offer—he abandoned his post to sample a few complimentary cocktail sausages from a nearby display.

I guess I shouldn't have taken it personally, but I did. For a couple of longtime associates who were supposed to be looking after me, they seemed very preoccupied with other interests.

On top of my more established troubles, I found this latest development very unsettling. I guess that's why I ended up stealing Harley Howard's deluxe limousine just a couple of days later. I really needed to drive around a little, clear my head and organize my thoughts.

It wasn't like I had to hot-wire the car or anything. Harley Howard's sweet ride was practically begging to be stolen. For one thing, the passenger side was unlocked. For another, I had discovered a set of keys inside a magnetized container that was hidden underneath one of the limo's front wheels. It's just like Uncle Andy always says: "Sometimes a burglar's greatest tool is other people's stupidity."

Don't get me wrong. I would have felt embarrassed if, say, Mrs. Halpern had spied the guy who opened pickle jars for her in possession of a stolen vehicle. On the other hand, I thought I'd be reasonably safe driving around in the early morning before I started my paper route. The streets of Snowflake Falls were practically deserted, and the windows of the limo were tinted black so that nobody could see who was driving.

I had already picked up my papers for delivery. I even had Gwenivere stashed in the trunk of Harley's limo. I figured there was plenty of time to drive around and think before I had to worry about my deliveries.

Of course, I wasn't counting on how totally great it felt to be steering something that didn't have a pink basket on the front of it. By the time I realized it was so late,

I had forgotten all about the way George Dial liked to stand in his living-room window and watch me deliver papers. At first, I only noticed George out of the corner of my eye. The next thing I did was very stupid. But I just kept thinking how George enjoyed humiliating me so much and how I wanted to make him envious. So I stopped in front of his house and rolled down the window of Harley's limo on the passenger side. When I knew he could see my face, I smiled and waved at him. Like I was just another friendly citizen of Snowflake Falls wishing him a great day. It was very gratifying to see George Dial's mouth fall open in complete and total awe.

My plan was to just keep going. But I was enjoying George's reaction so much that I hung around a few seconds too long. Meanwhile, George shot like a human cannonball out his front door in bathrobe, pajamas and slippers. Before I knew it, he had a death grip on the handle of the front passenger door and was pleading with me to unlock the door. I figured that George would attract some unnecessary attention unless I let him in. So I did. And then I just kept driving.

"Oh, man, I'm riding shotgun in old man Howard's Rich-mobile!" said George.

"You know this car?"

"Everybody in town knows this car," said George, who was practically vibrating with excitement. "You stole it, right? Don't worry. Nobody will care. Everyone hates Harley Howard—with the possible exception of Harley."

"Won't your gramma be worried about you, George?" I asked, trying to calm him down a little.

"She won't be up for another hour," he replied. He turned on the radio and began to listen to six different stations for a total of three seconds each.

"Don't get too comfortable," I cautioned, explaining that I still had to deliver my papers. "I've got to pull over and get Charlotte's bike out of the trunk."

"You're going to ride that toy-store excuse for transportation when we have genuine wheels?" shouted George.

"The point is to help me think," I said.

"No," said George. "The point is, you don't want to be late for your meeting with Ms. Pendergast."

George immediately offered to help me deliver my papers on the condition that I keep driving. I figured I was already late and had nothing to lose. So I just let Speed Dial take over my delivery. At first it was a bit weird. We would drive for maybe a few seconds until we got to a subscriber's house on the block. In fact, since the limo was so long to start with, sometimes we barely moved at all.

This did not discourage George, who would run up the steps of each house like a scared greyhound and set a paper on the step. If there was a cluster of subscribers on the same block, he would grab an armful of papers and hurl a couple of them toward adjacent porches. He never missed a porch once.

Not that Speed was exactly graceful or anything. Sometimes his bathrobe would loosen on the way back

203

from a delivery and it would start billowing behind him like a flannel cape. You could see the little race cars all over his pajamas. Once in a while, he would trip over a damp garden hose, which made his slippers squish loudly along the grass.

I don't think anybody noticed us. Except maybe Popcorn, who was so confused to see me driving a limo that he didn't even bark. But you know what? I was just happy that my ankle wasn't on today's breakfast menu. I guess that's why we kept driving around. "There's only one thing a cool chick likes better than a bad boy," a thrilled George observed. "And that's a bad boy in a hot car."

I could see George looking at me with newfound respect. He pointed out that—thanks to stealing Harley's limo—we had finished my route in record time. "You know what I like about you?" he asked. "You have this natural ability for solving honest problems in a totally dishonest way," he said. "Why not make that ability work for us?"

"Us? What do you want, George?"

"Now that you mention it, I have a little proposition for you," he said. After pausing for dramatic effect, he said, "If you accept, I will promote you from Grease Pig. Plus, I will sweeten the deal by giving you the supereasy midnight to two-AM drive-thru shift from Friday to Sunday. Since one of our most senior employees is working the shift, your total responsibilities will fall under the category of sleeping in the cot in my office."

"What do I have to do?" I asked suspiciously.

"Simple," said George, whose eyes lit up with fiendish glee. "We are going to steal the Devil's Dumpster."

I was so shocked that I had to pull over and park the limo. "The Devil's Dumpster from the Monster Truck Extravaganza?" I exclaimed. "Why would you want to steal that?"

"Because I want to drive the coolest vehicle on earth," he replied. "I want to experience the joyride to end all joyrides!"

"No way, George," I said. "I only stole this limo to organize my thoughts."

I guess George could see that I was weakening. Because he moved in for the kill. "There's something else," he confessed, his face turning bright red. "I have a totally hopeless crush on Nat."

"But Nat hates you," I observed, before I could stop myself.

"That's only because she hasn't seen my cool side," said George.

"And how do you propose to show her your cool side?" I asked.

"By cruising past her house in the Devil's Dumpster," answered George. "I promise we'll only stick around long enough to honk at her and wave."

"What about Nat's parents?" I asked. "What are they going to do when they see you drive up in a stolen vehicle?"

George explained that Nat's parents were good friends with his gramma. "They play bridge together every Friday night at the community center," he said. "When Lloyd's in town, he plays bridge too. The only person who'll be home is Nat."

I looked at George Dial's earnest face. He blushed even deeper every time he said Nat's name. "We're just borrowing Lloyd's truck from my gramma's personal garage," he said. "You think my own gramma's gonna toss me and my best friend in jail?"

I was going to argue about being George's best friend, but he looked at me and said, "Don't make me beg, man. Speed Dial is seriously in love."

I don't know why I finally said I'd do it. Maybe it was the fact that I can never resist a challenge. Or maybe it was the thought of no longer being a lowly Grease Pig. It could even be that I felt sorry for the love-struck Speed Dial. But mostly it was the fact that part of me really did want to steal the Devil's Dumpster. Because some opportunities only come your way once in a lifetime.

On the way back to return Harley's limo, George Dial thanked me for what he called my "totally unsavory but awesome car-theft skills." Then he looked at me like I was his best buddy in some cheesy war movie. "If anything goes wrong, I swear I won't leave you hanging," he said. "I'll take the bullet for the entire mission."

Over the next few days, George was so happy he never even caught a glimpse of Russell the imaginary rat. As for me, I was back delivering papers on Gwenivere.

You'd think that I would be happy since Mr. Wingate had finally convinced the Nutley brothers to begin working on the spare room again at double-overtime rates. But George was driving me crazy. He even organized a private strategy session for what he called "the heist." His whole strategy boiled down to making sure Charlotte knew nothing about our plans to steal the truck. "She'd ruin things faster than a flat monster tire," he said. Knowing Charlotte, it seemed like a very sound strategy.

On the night we went to steal the truck, George was dressed all in black. He looked like an undersized commando trying to remain inconspicuous in front of his gramma's double garage. I was dressed my regular way, which really seemed to disappoint him. "Are you sure you weren't followed?" he whispered.

"Will you relax?" I said. "I snuck out while Charlotte was reading her book on haircuts."

Everything went very smoothly at first. It was no problem getting into the garage. I was hoping that maybe the keys would be inside the Devil's Dumpster. Of course, they were not. But the truck was unlocked, so I popped the hood and took a look at what I had to deal with.

Fortunately, Cookie had trained me very well when it came to disabling all sorts of anti-theft elements—car alarms and the like. Luck was on our side in another way too, because the Devil's Dumpster was not what you would call overburdened with security features. After all, there are not a whole lot of people waiting in line to steal what is more or less a tractor on steroids.

With its jacked-up wheels and oversized tires, the Devil's Dumpster was built for rolling around in huge mounds of dirt. It would probably handle like your average water buffalo. But this didn't stop George from breaking into a huge grin when I managed to get the engine started. "This is so sweet!" he said, almost shaking with excitement.

Since I was the one with the most driving experience, George agreed to let me drive the monster truck out of the garage. After we figured out how everything worked, we'd switch places so that George could drive past Nat's house and wave. Once I got into the driver's seat, I noticed several mysterious levers and switches that I decided to ignore.

George joined me in the shotgun seat and I drove the car slowly off the property. We weren't more than a few feet away when I heard him yell, "May day!" which was George's commando way of saying we were in trouble.

What was the problem? Charlotte was pedaling Gwenivere toward us as fast as she could. George was all for burning rubber and leaving her in the dust, but I told him it was too late. I pulled the truck to the curb, and we both got out.

Charlotte finally arrived, all out of breath. "I knew you were up to something!" she cried. She started to go on about how we were commandeering a vehicle without permission and how neither of us had a totally authentic driver's license.

Forgetting all about acting like a commando, George panicked and started blurting out the whole story. When he came to the part about Nat, Charlotte interrupted him. "You're doing all this for love?" she asked, her voice suddenly going dreamy.

I guess listening to Charlotte drone on about soul mates had paid off. Because George picked up on the dreamy-voice thing right away. "Yeah, this is definitely for love," he said, like Charlotte was some fish he was ready to reel in. "I definitely feel like Nat could be my, you know, soul mate."

From where I was sitting, it seemed as if George had found his true soul mate in his lust to drive the Devil's Dumpster. Much to my surprise, I don't think this mattered much to Charlotte. While I could see disapproval in her eyes, there was also a flicker of excitement in there as well.

It made me remember what she said about how flaunting the conventionally accepted rules of society might be "supremely exhilarating." Suddenly, I realized that she wasn't going to be a problem. "Come with us, Charlotte," I said.

"What on earth for?" she asked, like it was the furthest thing from her mind.

"Because it will be supremely exhilarating," I said. "Plus, you're exactly what this team needs. A reasonable person who can keep us focused on our mission of love."

She thought about it for a second. But I wasn't worried in the least. I had seen Charlotte's look in other people as well. It was the look of someone who just needed the right excuse to do the wrong thing. Sure, Charlotte was a romantic and all. And part of her may have even wanted to come along just to make sure we didn't violate any crosswalk monitor rules. But I could also tell she wanted to try breaking the rules. Just to see what it felt like.

"All right, I'll go with you," she decided. "But you'll notice I'm not taking off my helmet."

The cargo area of the truck was all buttoned up with a special tarp that looked a bit like a trampoline. But George was so happy that he offered to put Gwenivere on what looked like a bike rack that was positioned just below the window of the Devil's Dumpster.

"Are you sure that's a bicycle rack?" asked Charlotte.

"It's either a bicycle rack or a gun rack," said George. "But I'm reasonably confident it works for both."

George and Charlotte started to argue about where to put her bike until I cut them off. "We can't stand here arguing," I told them. "Let's go."

George told Charlotte to chill because he knew exactly how the bike/gun rack worked. He was so sure that he took Charlotte's bike and fit it right onto the rack. Charlotte saw this as a convenient opportunity to get into the seat beside me. This irritated George, who declared, "Hey, I had first dibs on riding shotgun!" But one look at Charlotte's face was all it took to make him climb in the backseat.

We began chugging down the street like a turtle on big rubber wheels. But once we started inching forward,

George got so excited he was practically hyperventilating. "Rock 'n' roll!" he shouted, turning his fists into waving steer horns in a way that reminded me of the hats at Top Kow. Even though Charlotte pretended to be disgusted, I could see she was having fun too.

Things were going reasonably well until we got close to Nat's house. George insisted that he take the wheel so that he could show Nat how cool he was. Even though this was part of our agreement, I didn't really want to let him do it. Of course, George started bragging about how he had driven his gramma's lime-green Volkswagen around the deserted supermarket parking lot at least a dozen times.

That's when Charlotte spoke up. "George Dial may be the biggest dork in Snowflake Falls," she said, "but even a dork deserves a chance at the wheel."

That's how a grateful George ended up driving the Devil's Dumpster. Right away, I knew it was a terrible idea. He started fooling around with all the different switches and levers. When I told him to stop, he got this maniacal gleam in his eye. "Who's driving here!" he barked.

George managed to lurch down the street and—thanks to some holy miracle by the gods of transport—park across from Nat Wosney's house. Unfortunately, he noticed that the truck's horn was programmed to play the opening notes of three different popular songs about Satan. George chose the opening notes of a song called "The Devil Went Down to Georgia." It was loud enough to make Charlotte scream in total surprise.

In fact, blasting the first three notes of "The Devil Went Down to Georgia" was loud enough to make almost everyone in the neighborhood race to their front windows— including Nat. When George saw that Nat was watching, he began waving and yelling like the most lovesick geek in the entire universe. "Hey, baby," he screeched. "Wanna ride with the man?"

Nat came running out of the house like she was being chased by Russell the rat. "George Dial, have you gone totally insane?" she yelled.

George just shot her his goofiest grin. "Hey, Nat," he shouted. "Watch this!" Then he put the Devil's Dumpster into a hard reverse. Later, George told me that he meant to back up before doing a nice, smooth swing into Nat's driveway. But that's not the way it worked out. He backed up so hard that the rear wheels of the truck went right over the curb opposite Nat's house. After this unexpected turn of events, George freaked out.

He put the truck in drive and gathered a surprising amount of momentum while heading for the general direction of Nat's driveway. Unfortunately, George was so nervous that he somehow managed to trigger the giant dirt shoveler at the front of the truck. It began to move up and down as we headed for Nat's house, blocking the front windshield just long enough for the Devil's Dumpster to end up on Nat's front lawn.

The dirt shoveler moved down very quickly after that. Just like it was trying to dig itself through the pit of hell.

Unfortunately, it confused the pit of hell with a major chunk of the beautiful flower garden in front of Nat Wosney's house. The truck wasn't damaged and Nat's actual house was okay. But there were huge tire tracks on the lawn. And the flower garden was ruined.

"Oh, man," said George, who looked somewhat dazed. "We are totally hooped."

I made them both get out of the cab while I backed the truck off the lawn as best as I could. I was doing okay until I heard Charlotte, George and Nat yelling something at me. I didn't know what they were talking about until I got out of the truck and saw that I had run right over Charlotte's bike with the back wheels of the truck. Gwenivere was crushed like an old beer can.

"How did that happen?" I asked, totally shocked.

"It's the weirdest thing," said Nat, who sounded like she was numb. "The bike went flying off the rack while George was driving and slid off the tarp and onto the lawn." We all just stood there looking at the tire tracks on the lawn, the ruined front garden and Charlotte's crushed bike.

I thought Charlotte was going to cry or something. But the next thing she did totally surprised me. "Henry, you have to get out of here now," she insisted. "This is a violation of your probation for sure."

I just stood there as Nat lit a shaky cigarette right in the middle of her front lawn. "You better listen to her, Henry. My parents are going to be home any minute."

George added, "Do it, man! Just get out of here. I'll cover for you."

And so I did what I always did best. I ran. I ran without giving another thought to George or Charlotte or Nat. I ran just like the thief I was.

Later that night, I couldn't get to sleep no matter how hard I tried. So I managed to get the cell phone out from under my pillow on the first ring, while Oscar snored away.

"Guess what?" said the voice on the phone. "I finally finished that puzzle with all the leaves."

FOURTEEN

That's my one and only uncle for you. He never says "I love you" or anything like that. But I knew that telling me he finished The Majesty of Cape Cod was his way of saying he missed me. He explained that he couldn't talk long because he was using the warden's phone after lights-out as an extra special favor for good behavior. "I am still a guest of the government for two more weeks," he said. Then he told me how Wally and Cookie had told him that I was becoming a model citizen of Snowflake Falls.

I didn't want to tell Uncle Andy that his information was seriously out of date. So I replied that it was odd to see Wally and Cookie around town and not be able to say hi. Uncle Andy told me I sounded strange.

"You are okay, right?" he asked. "I mean you didn't break into anybody's house and get caught waxing the floor or anything?"

Since my Uncle Andy likes to fret behind bars, I lied and told him I was just fine. Then I threw in a bit of the absolute truth. "Everybody waves at me here," I said. "I just miss you. That's all."

"Don't worry, Henry," said Uncle Andy. "I have a plan that cannot fail."

"You're going to get me out of here?" I asked hopefully.

"Not exactly," he replied. "I'm coming to town to join Cookie and Wally as soon as I get sprung."

"That's great!" I said, almost waking Oscar up. "Then we can go home?"

"What home, Henry?" Uncle Andy's voice shifted into a whisper. "Listen, I'm going to get there in a couple of weeks. But you gotta pretend you don't know who I am."

"You too?" I asked. "What's going on?"

"We're going to rent that empty hardware store you wrote me about."

"You're going straight?" I asked, trying to imagine Uncle Andy and the others giving up their criminal ways to sell overpriced screwdrivers and extension cords. "Because Biggie's Bargin Barn will kill you."

"No, we're not going straight!" said Uncle Andy, as if he was totally allergic to the idea of making an honest living.

"I'll explain the whole thing when I get there." There was another pause on the line. "Henry?" he said softly.

"What?" I asked.

"Never mind," he replied, softer still. "I'll see you in a couple of weeks." Then the line went dead and all I could hear were Oscar's snores.

Uncle Andy had given me a lot to think about. But mostly my mind was on the whole stolen-truck incident. I guess Charlotte was thinking about it too. Early in the morning, she came into Oscar's room in her bunny bathrobe. She told me not to turn on the light. But I could still see that she had been crying, because her eyes were all swollen. "I just want you to know that I won't turn you in," she said.

"Why not?"

"Because we're friends." She looked at me with her swollen eyes. "We are friends, aren't we, Henry?"

I thought about this for a while. "I don't deserve a friend like you, Charlotte."

"Yes, you do," she insisted. "Can I tell you something stupid?" As usual, Charlotte didn't wait for my answer. "Sometimes, I think I bug you on purpose," she explained. "Just to test you, to see if you'll go away." She didn't talk for a while. Then I heard her say, "Even though I don't really want you to."

"There are way stupider things than that," I offered, trying to make her feel better.

"I wouldn't confess this to anybody else," she said. "But I actually liked riding in that truck with you and George. Even though it was totally wrong and against all my principles and everything."

"You could turn me in," I said. "I wouldn't hate you for it."

"You wouldn't exactly like me for it, would you?" she asked.

"What's that got to do with anything?"

"All my life I've been doing the right thing," she answered. "Not just doing the right thing, but telling everybody else to do the right thing. And what has it gotten me?" Even in the dark, I could tell that she might start to cry. "You're the only one who wants to eat with me in the cafeteria," she said. "Don't you think I know that?"

"I thought you didn't care what other people think."

"I lied," she said. "I lie about all sorts of things." She looked at her brother snoring in his supercrib. "You know what else?" she said, gently running her fingers through her Oscar's wispy hair as he slept. "He makes me so jealous I could spit."

I didn't know what to say so I changed the subject. "I'm really sorry about Gwenivere," I said.

"That's okay," she said, trying to hide the sadness in her voice. Then she opened the door to leave. The last thing I heard her say was, "I'm getting too old for that kind of bike anyway."

In the morning, George and Charlotte and I attended a special meeting about the stolen truck. The meeting was attended by the Wingates, Mr. and Mrs. Wosney and George's gramma, Winifred. Lloyd "Digger" Finster was also present. Lloyd was wearing a necktie and his red leather jacket with yellow flames shooting up the sleeves. Like his whole jacket was about to catch fire.

The meeting was led by Judge Messler, who called it "an official court proceeding held to determine some pertinent facts." Unfortunately for me, some of those facts concerned the violation of my probation. So I figured it was a good idea to listen very carefully.

Judge Messler, a very serious guy who looked a little like a bulldog around the jowls, was a close friend of all the families. "I think I know all of you here," he said. And then he stared a little at me and added, "Well, most of you anyway."

George looked like he was going to be sick. And Charlotte appeared very pale and even shorter than usual. She looked like she was going to burst into tears. Come to think of it, so did George. George's gramma had one of those hairstyles that made her look like she was wearing a beehive on top of her head. Underneath the beehive, she looked very upset.

I looked at the Wingates, and they were just sitting there, not saying much. Even Oscar knew something was up. He kept chewing on his lower lip and saying nothing at all. I tried not to stare at the Wingates, but it was impossible not to.

With their rocket-scientist glasses, they looked like some supersmart family that had stumbled into the wrong room.

"You have a very interesting background, Mr. Holloway," said the judge.

I didn't know what to say, so I just said, "Thank you, Your Honor."

"Have you ever hot-wired a car before?"

"Yes, sir." And just because I wanted to be totally truthful, I added, "Several times."

"Did you hot-wire Mr. Finster's vehicle?"

"Yes, sir."

"Who's idea was it to do so?"

I looked at the Wingates and the Dials and something came over me that I can't quite explain. It was a feeling that I thought might go away at any second. So, before it did, I thought I better jump right in. "The whole thing was my idea from start to finish," I said. "Charlotte kept begging me to take it back. The only reason she was there in the first place was to make sure George and I were wearing our seatbelts."

I couldn't believe I'd confessed to the whole thing. It pained me a great deal to admit it, but even though Uncle Andy was on his way to Snowflake Falls on some kind of secret hardware-store mission, I actually did not want to be run out of town.

I was thinking that had I made a very big mistake when the judge asked, "And what was George's role in all this?"

For a second, I was about to dump the whole thing on George's lap. Then I looked at him, with his mad-scientist hair flying off in all directions and without his pretend racing jacket. I guess I just couldn't help myself. "George had nothing much to do with it," I said. "I convinced him to come along at the last minute."

"Is that the truth, George?" asked the judge.

George looked at his gramma and said, "More or less." Then his eyes started to dart around like he was really nervous. He took a deep breath. And—in a very weak voice— said, "I think I want to man-up."

"Excuse me?" said the judge.

"Actually, Henry and I planned the whole thing together," he said. And then, his eyes darted around a little more and he added, "Actually, it was really my idea. But Henry's right about Charlotte. She was just along for the ride."

Suddenly, Charlotte stood up in her vice-principal's suit. "I object!" she exclaimed, like she was a big-time lawyer. "I'm just as much to blame as Henry or George." And then she looked down at the floor and said, "I'm deeply ashamed and feel I deserve to be punished."

"I see," said the judge. "I'd like to see all the interested adult parties in my chambers, please."

They were in his chambers for a long time. In the meantime, Charlotte, George and I sweated it out in another room. The room had a table with a stack of magazines, including some about the latest cars and trucks. But George was so nervous he didn't even look. Charlotte was trying to calm down by looking at her big book of haircuts. But I could tell it wasn't working.

Thankfully, the judge decided to be lenient on all three of us. This was mostly on account of the fact that Mr. Finster refused to press charges. Also George's gramma had agreed to pay for all the damages to the Wosney property. The judge took into consideration that George gave blood and was Employee of the Month at Top Kow Burgers five months running. "And let's face it," the judge said, "nobody who knows Charlotte Wingate is going to confuse her with some evil criminal mastermind."

The judge even ruled that "despite the special circumstances of Henry Holloway," I was to stay in Snowflake Falls and "continue my program of rehabilitation." He noted in my official report that Henry not only took full responsibility for his actions but—from all indications—was willing to take the blame for the irresponsible actions of others.

The upshot is that all three of us were sentenced to perform community service hours. The first thing we had to do was fix up the Wosney front garden. We also had to pick up litter on the highway. It seemed like everybody felt great about this but me.

Charlotte felt great because she was getting punished, which eased her conscience about the whole joyriding incident. Also, I think she actually enjoyed the work the judge assigned us. For one thing, it gave her the chance to boss George and me around. Of course, Charlotte referred to it as "supervision." But it still made me want to take a shovel full of dirt and decorate her nice white running shoes.

As for George, he was wearing his new bad-boy status like it was some kind of very expensive cologne. He had a whole new lease on life. "People look at you differently after you've walked on the wild side," he said. "I have gone from George Dial, social outcast, to Speed Dial, danger junkie."

While George was exaggerating as usual, I noticed that the gang at Top Kow Burgers was lightening up on him quite a bit. They stopped just short of telling him that Russell the rat was totally imaginary. Even Nat was being a little nicer to him. "Can you believe that little twerp rolled down the window and called out, 'Hey, Baby'?" she said. She always made sure to sound very sarcastic. But I could tell she was secretly flattered.

I guess word had gotten around that I had tried to take the blame for the whole Devil's Dumpster incident. Or maybe the gang at Top Kow Burgers was just bored. Anyway, they sprayed the entire surface of one of the Top Kow caps with gold paint and brought it out on one of the server trays. You know, like it was some valuable artifact from the tomb of King Tut or something. "Henry Holloway," said Stuart. "For services above and beyond the duties of Grease Pig, we hereby present you with the highest honor at the Snowflake Falls branch of Top Kow Burgers. The coveted Order of the Golden Horns."

Everybody started bowing like I was some pagan idol in an old adventure movie. Even Wiley got into it. "I will try to remain my humble Grease Pig self," I said. Of course, they made me put on the hat. I looked even more ridiculous than usual.

George didn't participate in the awards ceremony. On the other hand, he didn't put a stop to it either. Away from work, he made a big deal about how I "took a bullet" for him in court and he did his best to ease my Top Kow duties. He even hired a new kid to take over as Grease Pig. "When things slack off a little here, I will put you on the graveyard drive-thru shift," he said. "Just like I promised."

Much to my surprise, the Wingates didn't make a big deal about the stolen-truck incident. One day when I was helping Mrs. Wingate scrub Oscar's latest masterpiece off the wall, she smiled at me. "Sometimes I don't think there's enough adventure in my life, Henry." She sighed. "Does that sound selfish?"

I told Theodora that she was probably the most unselfish person in town. Then I asked her if she had ever done anything truly adventurous. Her eyes began to gleam behind her fake glasses. She explained that when she was first going out with Mr. Wingate, he would rent a convertible sports car for the entire afternoon. "We were just teenagers," she said wistfully. "I used to ride in the front seat with the wind in my hair and pretend I was a movie star."

Talking about her youth seemed to lift Mrs. Wingate's spirits. She actually started to whistle while scrubbing

Oscar's drawing off the wall. To be absolutely honest, it made me feel kind of good.

Maybe I was in an okay mood because the Nutley brothers were working very fast and getting closer to finishing my room. Or maybe I just felt guilty about turning Mrs. Wingate's only daughter into an official accomplice. But I decided to do another good deed and look through Charlotte's book of haircuts with her.

"You really want to?" asked Charlotte, who couldn't believe her good fortune.

"I will even tell you my favorite haircut," I said. It felt good to make Charlotte happy, even though Gwenivere was still out of commission.

Mind you, life in Snowflake Falls still had its downside. Since squashing Gwenivere with the Devil's Dumpster, I had to deliver my papers on foot. The only good thing about this was that Popcorn stopped chasing me. At first he'd growl when I came near the porch. But, after a while, his tongue just sort of hung out whenever he saw me. Mr. Kurtz said this was because I now had the Popcorn seal of approval.

But if Popcorn thought I was okay, Harley Howard was still enjoying taunting me with the idea of his hidden riches. One day as I was reading to him from *The Count of Monte Cristo*, he kept asking me if I was curious about any secret treasure he kept in the house. "It could be gold bars," he cackled, while daring me to try and crack his security code. "Stacks and stacks of them."

Of course, I realized that the old man wanted me to fail so that he could have the pleasure of making me his personal slave. But much as I disliked his teasing, his cigar smoke was even worse. I politely asked him to stop blowing smoke in my face many times. But he just said, "These are very expensive cigars from Havana. And one of the few pleasures I have left." Translation? Tough luck, Henry.

I tried to get back at him by reading the most obscure Elizabethan poems from The Universal Library of Immortal Literature. But no matter what I selected, or how badly I decided to mispronounce words, Harley Howard was surprisingly content. In fact, every time I deliberately stumbled on a phrase, Harley would break out in a big grin. "Let us pause to examine your ignorance," he would say.

But then something happened that was so awesomely monumental it made me forget all about Harley Howard. For once, I was walking downtown without Charlotte or George tagging along. I spotted a big new banner over the abandoned hardware store. It read *Opening Soon! Hercules Hardware and Security! We sell more than hardware. We sell peace of mind!*

But it wasn't the sign that got me so excited. It was the person I saw through the big picture window. It was none other than Wally Whispers, sweeping the floor. I guess I must have stood there in front of the window with my mouth hanging open for a good while. To tell you the truth, I was expecting Wally to ignore me as usual. Instead, he unlocked the door and addressed me on the street. "You are the boy who is here seeking part-time employment?" he whispered. "Why don't you come in so we can discuss your future in the thrilling world of home security?"

As soon as I got inside the store, Wally closed the blinds so that you couldn't see anything from outside. First, he apologized for ignoring me so much. He told me that he was busy getting used to his new identity. "I am now none other than Ernest T. Stubbs." He smiled. "And I have the official identification to prove it."

"Pleased to meet you, Mr. Stubbs," I said very seriously.

"You can call me Ernie," said Wally. "Now let us meet a few of your potential co-workers."

When we got to the back room, I could see Cookie. But there was one person I wanted to see most of all. He looked a little skinnier and had grown a scratchy beard. But it was none other than my one and only Uncle Andy.

My Uncle Andy isn't much for showing his feelings. But I guess he missed me so much that he had to give me a hug. "We were just going to get in touch with you," he said. Naturally, I wanted to know what this was all about. "It is about the letters you wrote me concerning life in Snowflake Falls," he said. "It got me very interested in the place. I especially liked your last couple of letters about getting to know Harley Howard. That's how I got the idea about the job."

"What job?" I asked. And then I suddenly realized what was happening. "You're going to rob Harley Howard."

"Not just Harley Howard," whispered Wally. "We're going to rob the entire town."

"Well, maybe not the entire town," corrected Uncle Andy modestly. "Just as many houses as we can infiltrate in one night."

When I said that I didn't understand, my uncle explained that it all started when he saw this old movie they showed in prison. "It's about a gang of thieves who open a store right next to the town bank," he explained. "The store is a place that sells luggage."

"But the gang is not really interested in the luggage-selling business," said Cookie. "What they are really interested in is building an underground tunnel that leads straight into to the bank vault next door."

"But the Snowflake Falls bank is two blocks from this location," I said.

"We are not going to build a tunnel to the bank," said Uncle Andy. "But we are going to pretend to be upstanding businessmen who are deeply concerned with the security needs of the locals."

"We are going to be so concerned with their security needs that we are going to supply them with everything from locks to alarms at an irresistible discount," said Cookie. "As well, we will do all the installing for next to nothing."

"Since we will have copies of the keys and help set the security codes, it will be a walk in the park to rob the unsuspecting citizenry," said Wally.

"But how many people are going to actually buy new locks and security alarms?" I asked. "This is a pretty sleepy town."

"That's why we start a little crime wave of our own making first," said Uncle Andy. "Nothing major. Just enough to get a little healthy panic going to increase sales."

"We will also offer free estimates for homes and businesses who are merely considering updating their security needs in the light of increased criminal activity," said Wally. "Naturally, this will require a close inspection of the premises."

"We figure we will have everybody set up for a mass burglary around Christmas," said Uncle Andy. "You know, hit everyone at once and then leave town with the cash and merchandise before anyone gets wise."

"We will be like Santa Claus," explained Cookie. "Only in reverse."

"Lenny has agreed to take pretty much whatever we can get our hands on," added Wally. "Even though he will rob us like a thief on the exchange, it is still a sweet deal."

"But how can you make sure people are going to be away from their homes all at once?" I asked.

"We need to work our job around some large-scale holiday event," said Uncle Andy. "Something that will serve as a distraction for our needs."

"With this in mind, we have been busy becoming acquainted with the social scene of Snowflake Falls," said Wally. "We've decided to pull the job during the holiday sing-along on Boxing Day."

"But Harley Howard never goes to the sing-along," I said. "How are you going to rob the richest man in town, if he refuses to leave his mansion?"

"This could be a problem," said Cookie.

Then Uncle Andy asked Wally and Cookie to leave the room. "I want to have a little talk with Henry," he said. When everyone else had left, Uncle Andy looked at me sheepishly. "Since you know this town, I might need your help with pulling off this job." He looked at me very seriously and asked, "Is there any way you can get Harley Howard to attend that sing-along?"

"I don't know," I said. "There might be. But he's very stubborn."

"I wouldn't even ask," said Uncle Andy. "Except this is for us. You and me."

I asked him what he meant, and he got all excited. "I was looking on the Internet and found this house we could rent in Arizona," he said. "It's perfect for us. All we need is the stake from this one last job and we can all live together like we used to."

"How much are you going to take?"

"Just enough for a new start," said Uncle Andy, who said the profit margin was going to be genuinely modest after covering expenses. "There's all the stock we have to buy for the store to make it look like a legitimate business. Plus the moving truck we have to rent to haul all the goods away. "

"Are you sure the job is worth it, Uncle Andy?"

"We're small-time crooks, Henry," he said. "And what is the first rule of a small-time crook?"

"Think small," I said. Then I told him he looked a little tired.

"Serial incarceration is beginning to lose its charm," he commented. "To tell you the truth, I've been thinking of going straight after this job."

"You mean you're never going to steal again after this?"

"Like I said, I just want a fresh start," he answered. "For both of us." Then Uncle Andy pepped right up again and gave me a big smile. "So what do you say, Henry? Are you in?"

I knew that I'd probably never get to live with Uncle Andy if Judge Barnaby had his way. "No problem, Uncle Andy," I said. "I'll do anything you want."

"You really had me going about the Hendersons, you know." He grinned. "Maybe you're more of a natural at this business than I thought." Then he looked at me as if he was going to ask something very important. "You haven't made any real friends around here, have you?"

I thought about how Charlotte and George looked up to me. I thought about how Oscar liked to throw his arms around my ankle and laugh while I dragged him around the house. I thought about how Theodora trusted me even though I didn't really deserve it. And then I thought about the gang at Top Kow and the people who were always waving to me on the street.

"No," I said. "I don't have a single friend in this town." It was the first time I had ever lied to my Uncle Andy since making up the Hendersons. But he didn't seem to notice. "That's good," he said. "Because nothing messes up a job faster than stealing from friends."

FIFTEEN

U ncle Andy told me it was very important to keep things as normal as possible while the various stages of the job were executed. "The most important thing to remember is that I am temporarily no longer your Uncle Andy," he said. "For the time being, my name is Andrew Tait."

Although my uncle looked different—thanks to growing a very respectable-looking beard—it was hard to think of him as anything but Uncle Andy, even though, like me, he had a lot of fake IDs. Still, I did my best to keep up with my usual routine. At times, it seemed as if nothing had changed. But then one day I opened the local paper and saw the headline *Crime Wave Hits Snowflake Falls*. Mind you, the crime wave was only three or four small robberies. But it was enough to give business for the new hardware store quite a boost.

You should have seen Wally Whispers behind the counter of the hardware store, talking locks and keys with the locals like he'd been doing it all his life. He even made up free keychains with the store's logo and passed them out to one and all. One afternoon, I watched him for a while. He spent ten minutes helping Sylvia decide between a beige electrical outlet cover and a brown one. "Thank you, Ernie," said Sylvia. "Your sense of color is a lifesaver."

If I didn't know better, I would almost think that Uncle Andy and his associates were enjoying pretending to be honest businessmen. I could tell that Uncle Andy was enjoying it a bit too much. It all started with the Welcome to Snowflake Falls Committee. The head of the committee was none other than Ms. Penelope Pendergast, who took an immediate liking to Mr. Andrew Tait.

Soon I began to hear rumors that they were dating. Then I noticed that Ms. Pendergast was starting to knit a red sweater. Red just happens to be my uncle's favorite color.

I asked Wally about it in private, and he got very serious. "I have never seen your uncle so smitten," he said. "It is like Cupid has hit him over the head with a giant sledgehammer."

I began to see Uncle Andy and Ms. Pendergast walking around town as if they were on the longest date in the history of Snowflake Falls. At first, I wasn't too concerned. But then I saw the two of them coming out of the movies, holding hands.

I was so shocked that I went to see my uncle at the hardware store the next day. He took me into the stockroom for a private conversation. "I saw you holding hands with my school counselor last night," I said. "Right in the middle of a public street."

Uncle Andy blushed. "We were coming out of this horror movie about a giant bug," he said. "She was just a little scared, that's all."

"I am very fond of Ms. Pendergast," I pointed out. "She bakes me fresh muffins five days a week."

"She talks about you all the time," said Uncle Andy. "And she doesn't even know we're related." He gave me a lovesick grin before adding, "Penelope is very dedicated to keeping you on the straight and narrow."

"Your relationship is becoming the talk of Snowflake Falls," I said. "There are all sorts of rumors flying around."

"What kind of rumors?"

"That you and Ms. Pendergast are going to make your own raspberry jam and enter it in the homemade jam contest at the Pumpkin Festival," I said. "Mrs. Halpern says this means you're practically pre-engaged."

"Pre-engaged?" said my uncle. "Just because we both like preserves?"

"I'm worried, Uncle Andy. Wally says you're smitten."

"Don't be concerned, Henry. Andrew Tait may be smitten to the core. But Andy Holloway is all business."

Wally and Cookie weren't so sure about Uncle Andy's state of mind. "This town can cast a very strange spell over a normally coldhearted individual," Cookie said. "Have you noticed that everyone is always waving at you, even when you don't wave back? I find this highly unnatural." I told Cookie to just return the wave and try to blend in. Pretty soon he was waving at one and all.

I watched as Cookie, Wally and Uncle Andy became die-hard Snowflakes. When preparations for the Pumpkin Festival began in October, they pitched right in. On the actual weekend of the festival, Cookie and Wally won the senior division of the three-legged race. And Uncle Andy outbid everyone for Mr. McHugh's prizewinning tomato, which was practically the size of a grapefruit.

They went on every ride and played every game there was. They brought four kinds of fresh-squeezed lemonade between them and shook hands with just about everyone in town. At one point, Wally asked if the man making animal shapes out of balloons wanted to take a little break. After that, he took right over and started to make what turned out to be a fairly decent balloon giraffe.

When Uncle Andy discovered that Ms. Pendergast was selling her homemade baked goods to raise money for the school band, he bought thirty-six blueberry muffins. I went up to him and whispered, "Have you forgotten that you're allergic to blueberries?" All he did was smile and say, "Would you like a muffin, Henry?"

All in all, you would have never guessed that these three individuals were planning a robbery of any kind. But then, it's funny how fast a career prisoner can get used to a place that doesn't have bars on the windows. Even though the hardware store was just a front, Uncle Andy developed an instant dislike for Biggie's Bargin Barn. "How is the little guy supposed to make a living in this town?" he asked, when he discovered that some people were buying their new locks at Biggie's.

"It is only our personal good fortune that we have dishonesty to fall back on," added Wally.

Cookie started to say that Biggie's was actually a very cheerful place. In fact, he was thinking of continuing to work there part-time. But Uncle Andy insisted that Cookie quit his job as a greeter at Biggie's if he was going to work at the hardware store. "There goes the least objectionable honest work I ever had," said Cookie.

Even Oscar could not resist the lure of Biggie's. One night at dinner, he kept looking around at everybody like some wheels were turning around in his little head. Finally, he opened his mouth to say his first whole sentence ever. "I like Biggie's!" he shouted.

Naturally, a grinning Oscar was expecting attention and approval. But there was only silence. Mr. Wingate, who had just gone over his store accounts that afternoon, turned very pale. "Excuse me, everyone," he said very formally. "I believe I'm going to lie down in the living room."

Theodora could not believe what she was hearing. "In the living room?" she asked.

Harrison nodded. "I do not wish to be disturbed," he said. Once Mr. Wingate had wandered off to lie down on the living-room couch, Charlotte spoke up.

"Can I be the one to wash out Oscar's mouth with soap?" she asked.

"Don't be silly, Charlotte," said Theodora. Then she kissed Oscar on the cheek and headed for the living room to check on Mr. Wingate.

"Oscar gets away with murder," grumbled Charlotte. She marched off in a huff, leaving me alone with Oscar, whose mouth was hanging open in puzzlement.

"Way to go," I said. "Your first whole sentence!"

Oscar shot me a grateful grin. "I like Biggie's!" he repeated.

The next day, I moved into the finished guest room at the Wingates. Mind you, I would have to keep my door closed since Oscar had finally graduated from his supercrib to a small bed without bars. I discovered that if I left the bedroom door open, he would wander in whenever he felt like it. But so what? I was still deliriously happy. At least at first.

Maybe it was all the silence that came with not having to listen to Oscar's constant snoring. There was nothing to distract me from wondering what everyone in Snowflake Falls would think of me once my uncle and his associates pulled off the big robbery. Of course, all of us would be on our way to Arizona by then. But I knew it wouldn't take long before they figured out I'd betrayed them all.

I guess maybe because I was feeling a little guilty, I lost my temper with Harley Howard. I had just finished reading him a poem by Robert Frost called "The Road Not Taken." It was all about this person reflecting on the choices he had made in life and whether he went down the right path.

It was the kind of poem that made you think. Exactly what I was doing when Harley Howard blew a stream of smoke in my face. After that, I really lost it. I started to tell him how my mother died of cancer and how I hated breathing in all his toxic cigar smoke. "Why didn't you say so?" said Harley, who immediately stubbed out his cigar. "What am I supposed to be? A mind reader?"

The old man was being quite reasonable, all things considered, but I was all wound up because of the cigar smoke and his superior attitude and the way he was always bragging about what a great security system he had. I couldn't take it anymore.

I knew that what I was about to do could really complicate Uncle Andy's plan for a smooth and easy robbery of Harley Howard's mansion. On the other hand, I just couldn't help myself. "I know your security code," I said. "I can stop your alarm from going off any time I want."

"Bullcrap," said Harley.

"How about if we do a little test right now?" I asked. "Two tries and I'll crack the code."

"One try," said Harley. "That's all you get. And when the alarm goes off, you can head straight for the toilet brush."

"If I win, I get a favor right? Any favor I want?"

"That's what I said, didn't I? I'm a lot of things, kid, but Harley Howard is no welcher."

The two of us went to the wall by the front door where the code panel was. Harley was looking very smug while activating his alarm system. "I'm going to enjoy this," he said. "I think I'll make you wear a frilly apron while you dust."

I got a little slip of paper out of my wallet and stared at it for a few seconds. I had two possible choices. And, if I made the wrong one, I'd be polishing Harley Howard's silverware until every last speck of tarnish was gone.

"What's the matter, kid?" said Harley. "Losing your nerve?"

I took a deep breath and made my choice. I could feel a trickle of sweat running down my forehead as I punched in the series of numbers. When I was done, there was no alarm. Only the sweet sound of silence.

Harley Howard was so shocked that he had to sit down. After a while, he said, "How did you do that?"

"All it took was a little research at the library," I said. "When it comes to security codes, most people use their birthdays."

"Keep talking," said Harley.

"I came across your birthday in an old copy of the *Flurry*," I explained. "That's where I found your wife's birthday too. I almost tried your birthday first. But I changed my mind."

"What made you change it?"

"All the pictures, I guess. I mean, you looked so happy together. You try to hide it. But I can tell how much you miss her."

After that, Harley was quiet for a while. Like he was lost in his own thoughts. Then he said, "Well, you got me. What favor can I do for you?"

"I want you to attend the holiday sing-along."

"Of all the favors you could ask for, why would you ask for that?"

"I have my reasons."

Harley thought for a while. "Okay, a bet's a bet. But I'm not going alone. You're coming with me."

"Why would you want to go with me?"

"Let's just say I have my reasons too."

Then Harley Howard got all quiet again. He got so quiet that I couldn't stand it. "Do you want me to read to you?" I asked.

"No," he said. "I feel like listening to some music for a while. There's a Sinatra record on the top of that stack. Put it on, will you?"

"I thought you said never to touch your record collection."

"Never mind what I said, Henry. Just do it," he said. "Keep the volume down low." Then he added, "Please."

I put the Sinatra record on the stereo and then put the old-fashioned needle on the old-fashioned record to hear it play. It was this song about being lonely in the middle of the night. When there was nobody else around to talk to or just be with. I'd never heard it before. But it kind of felt like I had.

I was about to leave when Harley said, "See you at the usual time on Wednesday."

"You want me to come back after all this?" I asked. "You're going to have to get a new alarm code and everything."

"Why?" asked Harley. "Are you planning on robbing me?"

"No," I said, trying to sound as convincing as possible.

"So there's no reason I shouldn't trust you, right?"

"Since you put it that way…"

"That's the way I'm putting it." And then, much to my surprise, he offered me a genuine smile. "I'll say one thing," he added. "Life around you is never boring." I was making my way toward the door when he spoke to me again. "Sorry about your mother," he said. I told him thank you. And then there was nothing but the sound of the record until I was too far away to hear it anymore.

I was reasonably sure Harley wouldn't change his alarm code, which would make things a lot easier for Uncle Andy and the guys. But if Harley's attitude was a bit unexpected, I was in for an even bigger surprise.

It all started a few days later when George officially put me on the midnight drive-thru shift on the weekends. George asked me if I could keep a secret. "Absolutely not," I replied.

"I'm serious, Henry," said George. "Nobody can know about what you're going to see on the graveyard shift except the three of us."

Before I could ask what George meant, Mr. Wingate came walking through the rear entrance in a long coat. "What are you doing here?" I asked.

"I work here," said Mr. Wingate, who took off his coat to reveal the full Top Kow uniform in all its bovine glory.

"What's going on?" I said.

"Harry will explain," said George. "I have work to do."

After George went back to his office, I said, "Harry?"

"He likes to call me that at work," said Mr. Wingate. "It's the least I can do." He reached under the counter and put on his official Top Kow cap. "George hired me with no fast-food experience whatsoever." I guess I was too shocked at the sight of Harrison Wingate in Top Kow horns to say much of anything for a while. Then out of nowhere, Mr. Wingate said, "It takes a very smart guy to hot-wire a truck like the Devil's Dumpster."

"It's a lot easier than most people think," I said.

"It's not that easy," observed Mr. Wingate.

"No offense," I said, "but how would you know?"

"Can you keep a secret?" he asked.

"Why does everybody in this town keep asking me that?"

Mr. Wingate gave a little laugh. Then he got very serious. "I used to steal cars," he said. "Just joyriding, mostly. I was desperate to impress Theodora back then."

"You stole that convertible she keeps talking about?" I exclaimed.

"Theodora never knew it was stolen," he explained. "After a while, she started dating some other guy. But I kept stealing cars."

"What happened?"

"I was sent to a juvenile facility," he said. "I met some counselors there who really turned me around. That's how I got back with Theodora. And that's why I became involved with the Second Chance program."

"I can't believe you were ever dishonest," I said as he got out the frozen hamburger patties. "You must need the extra money bad to be working here at this hour."

"You know that five-minute shopping spree for the person who draws the winning ticket?" said Mr. Wingate. "With promotion, merchandise and other expenses, it's going to cost us just about everything we've managed to save."

To tell you the truth, I was excited about the prospect of grabbing at merchandise without being sent to jail.

I guess Mr. Wingate could tell what I was thinking. Because right away he told me I wasn't eligible. "For one thing, you're a minor," he pointed out. "And for another, you're kind of like family."

I asked him why the prize was so extravagant. "You have to think big for this to work," he explained. "Besides, if I'm going to go bankrupt anyway, I might as well have a little fun."

"Does Mrs. Wingate know you're working here?"

Mr. Wingate shook his head. "She's a very sound sleeper," he said. "And she's usually out like a light by the time Oscar gets through with her." Mr. Wingate smiled affectionately, as if he knew he was lucky to have a wife like Theodora. "She's woken up a couple of times to find me gone. But I just told her I like to go for walks at night sometimes. You know, for the stress."

Then Mr. Wingate told me that if he had to shut down the store, he would probably have to take some sort of job at Biggie's.

"You really like this town, don't you?" I asked.

"It's my home, Henry."

"I just don't understand why everybody has to make a big deal about vegetable-growing competitions and sing-alongs."

"I noticed you ate your share of cotton candy at the Pumpkin Festival," said Mr. Wingate. "I also noticed that you bought a jar of raspberry jam from Ms. Pendergast and Mr. Tait. That was very nice of you, Henry."

"Well, I got a little caught up in Mr. Tait's enthusiasm when he won third prize," I said. "I've never seen a person so happy with taking third place."

Mr. Wingate smiled at me. "People in small towns are different," he explained. "You'd be surprised at the things they can get excited about." Mr. Wingate grinned. For the first time I could see a mischievous gleam in his eye behind the thick glasses. All of a sudden, it wasn't so hard to imagine him stealing cars.

"You're different here than you are at home," I said.

"In what way?" he asked. When I hesitated, he said, "Let's you and me be just a couple of co-workers right now, okay?"

I nodded. "I don't know," I said. "You seem more, you know, human."

Mr. Wingate looked down at his speckled cow vest so that I could see the tips of his Top Kow horns. "It must be the uniform," he said. Then he looked up and said, "I've been meaning to thank you for being so nice to Charlotte, Henry. It means a lot. To her and to me."

He cleared his throat. "I know it wasn't right for you to steal that truck," he said. "But I was very proud of you for standing up and taking your medicine like that. We all were." I could tell Mr. Wingate really meant what he said. In his uniform he looked like a very emotional cow.

Just then, we could hear someone placing a drive-thru order. Harrison Wingate went over to the speaker and happily repeated the customer's request. "Two TK Frosties?" he said. "Of course, sir. Do you want sprinkles with that?"

That night, I went to sleep in the brand-new spare room and thought about what would make a grown man work at Top Kow Burgers. I guess when you have a family, you have to make all sorts of humiliating sacrifices. But when all was said and done, you knew you were doing the right thing.

I thought about how the people of Snowflake Falls would remember me after I ran off with Uncle Andy to Arizona. Because I felt a little guilty, I began to hang out with George at his gramma's house. We watched a few of his favorite DVDs. I even called him Speed once in a while.

George's gramma was very happy to have me visit. "You're the first person he's ever brought to the house, Henry," she said.

George just grinned at his gramma and said, "I told you he'd come. That's how the Big H rolls." After that he started to call me Big H all the time. As in, "Pass the pretzels, Big H."

I guess, when it was all over, George would have a few other names for me. Like traitor and turncoat and a bunch of others I'd rather not contemplate. Then I started to think about Charlotte and how disappointed she would be. But maybe there was a way I could leave a taste of something good behind. Something that people would remember so they'd know I wasn't a totally bad guy.

I began to run through a short list of the most humiliating things that could happen to me. Then after a while, I stopped. Because I knew exactly what I had to do.

SIXTEEN

It took me a while. But finally I went up to Charlotte and said, "Okay, I'll do it."

"Do what?" she asked suspiciously.

"I'll let you give me a haircut."

I could tell Charlotte's previous experience at haircutting had left her skeptical. "And you won't run away until I tell you I'm finished?" she asked.

"I promise," I said, feeling a drop of sweat ease its way down my scalp. "You can even make me look like that Roman soldier if you want."

"You mean it?" she asked, all excited. "You'd do that for me?"

"Sure," I said. "Knock yourself out."

I thought maybe Charlotte would give me a bit of time to get used to the idea. But it turned out that she'd been waiting to use her new home-barber kit for quite some time. Plus, Harrison was at the store and Theodora was taking Oscar to an afternoon appointment with the pediatrician. "I think it might be best if we took advantage of the fact that we won't be interrupted," said Charlotte.

Charlotte turned her bedroom into a temporary hair salon. I sat in her pink desk chair while she put a plastic cape around my neck and covered her pink rug with newspaper. Unfortunately, I had an excellent view of some of the old dolls she had practiced her styling skills on. They looked like their hair had been pulled out by the roots before being pasted back on in the dark.

Not that Charlotte didn't have an interesting technique. It involved her opening the big book of haircuts and peering intently at the guy who looked like the Roman soldier. She started to make cutting motions with her scissors in midair, getting closer and closer to my actual scalp while looking at the picture in the book.

"Oww!" I said. "Watch my ear!"

"I haven't even touched you yet," she protested.

"Sorry, I thought I felt something."

"Don't talk. I have to concentrate to make sure both sides are symmetrical."

Charlotte moved her scissors back from my head and then zeroed in while snipping at a fast clip. Sort of like an airplane getting ready to land on the runway. I guess the scissors must have touched down eventually, because the next thing I knew there was a big pile of my hair on the newspaper. "I'm going to get the hand mirror now," said Charlotte. Like she was warning me to be prepared for a major change in appearance.

I thought I was ready for anything. But nothing could have prepared me for the image I saw in Charlotte's pink hand mirror. I looked like a guy who had accidentally thrown himself into the path of lawn mower that had managed to confuse his hair for a clump of grass. Looking into the mirror was a frightening thing. But, for some reason, I could not bring myself to look away.

"What do you think?" asked Charlotte, all eager for my opinion.

I put down the mirror and looked at the anticipation of my happy reply on her eager barber's face. I wanted to tell Charlotte that it was the most horrible haircut I had ever experienced in all my years of haircuts. I wanted to tell her that the only reason she should pick up scissors again was to cut open a bag of potato chips.

Then I remembered that I was going to leave town in a moving van filled with Christmas presents that didn't belong to me. Charlotte was going to think such terrible things that not even the fact I was never going to see her again could make up for it. With this in mind, I swallowed hard and thought about what to tell her. "I think the raw talent is there," I finally managed. "No question about that."

"I know it's a little uneven in spots," she admitted. "Maybe I should touch it up a bit."

"No, no," I urged. "I look Roman enough!"

"You really think so?" she asked.

"Oh, yeah," I lied. "All that's missing is a gladiator's sword." Then I took off the little plastic cape and said, "I almost feel like I should pay you."

"Thank you, Henry."

"For what?" I asked. "It'll probably all grow back." I shouldn't have mentioned that last part, but Charlotte didn't notice. She was too busy getting choked up. "You have proven yourself to be a true and faithful friend, Henry Holloway. I'll never forget you as long as I live."

All I could think of was that Charlotte was probably right. Even though there would come a time when she'd like to forget I ever existed.

It was not easy to go out in public the next day. The first thing Uncle Andy said when he saw me was, "What the heck happened to your hair?"

"It's a long story," I replied. I guess Uncle Andy didn't want to hear it. Mostly because he had the whole plan for the Boxing Day robbery weighing heavily on his mind.

Uncle Andy told me that, once they pulled off the job, they would get out of Snowflake Falls as fast as possible. They planned to rent a big moving van in order to haul away everything they stole. In a few days, they would send me some money and let me know where to meet them in Vancouver. "After that, we are all off to Arizona," he said. "Where the only thing we'll have to worry about is having enough suntan lotion."

My uncle knew I'd be busy at the sing-along with Harley Howard and would be unable to be any help during the robbery. He told me I'd helped enough by getting the combination to Harley's security alarm. "You're doing him a big favor," said Uncle Andy. "Except for his missing possessions, he'll hardly know we were there."

"What if he's changed the security code?" I asked.

"From what you told me, he won't," said Uncle Andy. "He trusts you."

While my uncle forbade me to actually participate in the robbery, he requested my technical advice on the best way to break into the houses on my paper route. "I know how your mind works, Henry," he said. "You have been checking things out while riding your girlfriend's bike."

"She's not my girlfriend," I protested. Uncle Andy apologized. And then we got down to business. I told him the best way to burglarize all the customers on my paper route. I felt surprisingly bad about the whole thing. Maybe that's why I asked Uncle Andy for a couple of special conditions.

I requested that he refrain from burglarizing the Wingates. "Done," he said.

"And don't touch Harley Howard's record collection."

Uncle Andy said, "Henry, he's a rich guy. And rich guys always have plenty of insurance."

"Just promise," I said. "It's the only thing he really cares about."

"Okay," said Uncle Andy solemnly. "I promise."

I apologized for cutting down on Uncle Andy's list of benefactors. He just shrugged. "It's this crazy town," he said. "It makes you want to do the right thing against your better judgment."

I asked him what he meant, and my uncle looked at me like he had a bad case of indigestion. "Good citizenship is spreading among my associates like some sort of terrible disease," he complained. "Everyone is forgetting their professional obligation to be objective."

He told me that Wally and Cookie had just given him a long list of people they couldn't bring themselves to rob. "All of a sudden, Wally can't steal from people who wave at him on the street, and Cookie can't steal from the friends he made as a greeter at Biggie's. How are we supposed to make a living?"

Uncle Andy informed me that this sudden outbreak of consideration was really cutting into the job's profit margin. "We can still make this job work," he said, "but I don't mind telling you that a lot of the fun's gone out of it." He sighed. "Even I can't bring myself to rob Penelope."

I felt so sorry for my uncle that I asked if there was anything I could do.

"Just don't tell me not to rob anybody else," said Uncle Andy. "We can't afford it."

Everyone in town was preoccupied with so many different things over the holidays that I figured Christmas would pass by without much of a fuss. This was what I was used to anyway. To tell you the truth, Christmas has never been all that special to me since my mother died. I'm not blaming my Uncle Andy. The holidays are always a very busy time for him, professionally speaking. And it's not that I don't miss the things my mother and I would do at Christmas. She used to call them "those special holiday moments." When she died, I figured those moments were long gone.

But thanks to the Wingates, I got more into the Christmas spirit that I ever thought possible. We drank eggnog and decorated the tree. We all had a good laugh when Oscar dumped a clump of tinsel on his head. Much to my surprise, I did really well in Christmas tips and bonuses from my paper route. Mr. Kurtz was especially generous because he said I put up with being chased down the street like a very mature individual.

We had a little after-hours Christmas party at Top Kow. Stuart and Lowell did an all-belch version of "God Rest Ye Merry Gentleman." Even George thought it was very festive.

Before I knew it, it was Christmas Eve. When everyone else was asleep, I snuck downstairs using my best burglary skills and put a few presents under the Wingate Christmas tree. I looked out the window and noticed that it was starting to snow. For a few minutes, I just stood by the window and watched the thick flakes cover the ground. I couldn't help thinking that Snowflake Falls never looked so good.

By the time I got to bed, it was quite late. Even so, it took me a long time to get to sleep. I kept worrying about whether Uncle Andy's Boxing Day burglary spree would go off without a hitch. I finally managed to get to sleep. When I woke up, it was early Christmas morning. The door of my room was open, and Oscar was curled up asleep at the bottom corner of my bed. His mouth was wide open, and he was making soft little piglike noises.

I noticed that he was clutching something tightly in his fist. I pried his fingers open very gently and discovered that he was holding one of my long-lost earplugs.

Oscar stirred slightly and then opened his eyes before breaking into his stupidest grin. "Hen-rrry!" he shouted. I took the earplug out of his sweaty hand and wished him a Merry Christmas. Then I picked him up and carried him into the living room. Just because I felt like it.

Everybody got a lot of neat presents. And I'm happy to say that Charlotte really liked what I got her. "Springtime in Paris!" she exclaimed. "Only the most elegant perfume ever!"

"It's slightly used," I cautioned. I waited for Charlotte to be all disappointed. But you know what? She turned the whole thing around like it was actually an advantage.

"That's even better," she said. "This way your gift has a mysterious romantic history."

"You know, it kind of does," I answered. "Maybe someday I'll tell you about it."

Charlotte got me a very interesting Christmas present. It was a black bike-racing helmet like all the big-time professionals wear. And it didn't have a single sticker on it. "I know you don't have a bike," she pointed out. "But the gift is really supposed to be metaphorical. Every time you look at it, I want you to remember to stay safe." As a gesture, it was typically Charlotte. But even though the gift was only metaphorical, I really appreciated the thought.

As a joke, Theodora got me my own special pair of Wingate rocket scientist glasses. "Don't worry, Henry," she said, shooting me a secret look. "The lenses are just plastic."

"Now you're officially one of us," said Charlotte. I put the glasses on and Mr. Wingate said he thought I looked very dignified. We took a group photo, and it looked like I fit right in. When Theodora saw how Oscar was squinting, she said, "I think we should take him to the optometrist."

The rest of Christmas Day was surprisingly good too. I went over to George Dial's house and watched this jet-pilot movie called *Top Gun*. It was way more fun than I thought it would be, even though George kept yelling, "I feel the need for speed!" every five minutes. So for his Christmas present, I told George that there was actually no Russell the rat. George was so happy that he threw his arms around me for a couple of seconds—forgetting his rule about not hugging guys unless they were mortally wounded in combat.

I even got a chance to sneak away and see Uncle Andy. He was wearing a very nice red sweater that was hand-knit for him by Ms. Pendergast. I think he felt bad because he went right out to the hardware store and got her a lamp that automatically clicked on and off when you clapped your hands.

"Do you ever wonder what Ms. Pendergast is going to think when we're gone?" I asked.

"She'll probably want to break the lamp I gave her over my head," said Uncle Andy.

I asked Uncle Andy why he kept scratching at the sweater Ms. Pendergast made him. "It itches," he said. "Plus, it's a little too small."

"So why don't you take it off?"

"I will," said Uncle Andy. But he kept right on wearing it.

You'd think after such a great day, I'd get a better night's sleep. But I was actually quite restless. I kept thinking about the upcoming burglaries. I was glad when Boxing Day came around and I could lose myself in all the celebration.

First, there was the Wingate Boxing Day Blowout Shopping Spree. There was a pretty good crowd for the raffle. I even saw none other than Cookie Collito. I went up to him as quietly as possible and whispered, "Pardon me, but aren't you supposed to be in plotting a burglary right now?"

Cookie looked embarrassed. "I snuck away for a few minutes," he said. "There's no way I was going to miss this. I bought five tickets!" I asked if there was a conflict of interest because he was a greeter at Biggie's. Cookie shrugged. "What do I care?" he whispered. "We are bound for Arizona shortly, are we not?"

As it turned out, it was fortunate that Cookie showed up. Much to his surprise, he drew the winning ticket. "I won!" he shouted. "I won the shopping spree!" After a whole series of bells and whistles went off, a few people in the crowd slapped Cookie on the back and said, "Congratulations, Donny!"

Cookie couldn't believe his luck. "It's like the whole town is giving me their permission to steal," he said.

That's how Cookie ended up racing around the store, throwing as many things as he could into a series of shopping carts. Toasters, electric blankets, a fistful of baby clothes. Just about anything he could grab. In fact, he didn't slow down until he came to a selection of holiday baked goods. Now, as we all know, Cookie is very particular about freshness. Even when he is getting things for free.

You may think that five minutes is not a long time. But it was long enough for Cookie to stockpile a surprising amount of free merchandise. As the grand prize winner, he had to pose for newspaper pictures with all his loot. Normally, Cookie avoids having his picture taken at all costs.

But for this special occasion, Cookie was more than happy to smile for the camera while holding a brand-new microwave oven. After that, he had to shake hands with a long line of well-wishers.

"I love this town," said Cookie, hugging his new microwave like it was a baby. And you know something? At that moment, I think he really did.

I was very happy for Cookie, but a little nervous about attending the sing-along with Harley Howard. Even though there was quite a bit of snow on the ground, it seemed that just about everyone in town was in the square and ready to have a good time.

Even Harley had a better time than he had anticipated. He had a pretty good singing voice, and I think he missed using it. He kept nudging me in the ribs and telling me to sing louder. At one point, he said, "You know, I didn't want to come. Now I don't want to go home." I imagined Harley's mansion stripped bare of everything but his records and thought, Maybe you shouldn't.

For me, the most awkward part of the whole evening was the unveiling of the big new sign that was going to replace the old one just outside of town. It had the new winning slogan on it: *Welcome to Snowflake Falls. Where Life Is As Friendly As Your Next-Door Neighbor.* The winner of the contest was none other than Ms. Penelope Pendergast who kept looking around for someone. My best guess? Uncle Andy.

I didn't know any of the following details until later when my uncle explained everything in a letter he wrote. It was a very long letter. I think Uncle Andy was still trying to figure out how everything went so wrong. I had to read it several times. Because every time I read it, I was even more surprised than the last time.

Here's what happened. At the time of the getaway, Uncle Andy was busy being nervous about driving the big moving van. Probably because it was full of stolen goods. He was even was more nervous about missing the ferry. So I guess that's why a couple of very unfortunate things happened. First, they had a flat tire. And then they got stuck in the snow. By the time they got everything fixed, they had missed the ferry.

Needless to say, they were very upset. Uncle Andy was still wearing the sweater Ms. Pendergast knit for him, and he kept scratching at it.

"Why don't you take off that scratchy sweater?" asked Wally Whispers. "It is torture just watching you scratch."

"Also the sweater is too short in the sleeves," said Cookie.

"It's not so bad if you wear a light shirt under it," said Uncle Andy.

"Enough sweater talk!" said Wally. "We cannot head for the ferry now. Word of the burglary could have reached the authorities."

"We should turn back," said Andy. "We can hide the van and come back for it later."

"But what if someone finds it?" asked Cookie.

"So what? They can't prove it was us," said Wally.

"Let's face it," said Cookie. "We are the likeliest suspects."

"What if we just hid the van and went back to town for a while," said Andy. "We could keep running the hardware store like nothing happened."

"With all due respect," said Cookie. "Has that sweater made you nuts?"

"Cookie has a point," said Wally. "Where does this stop? Why don't we just return the stolen merchandise like a bunch of good little tooth fairies?"

"Would that be so bad?" said Uncle Andy. "We could do it a little at a time. You know, like an installment plan."

Everybody was quiet for a while, until Wally Whispers said, "I am not altogether averse to the hardware business."

Then Cookie said, "May I remind everyone that we are professional crooks. Stealing is what we do. Besides, what about all those golf carts in Arizona?"

"I hear the dry heat can cause chafing," said Andy.

"Perhaps we should go back to town and sleep on it," said Wally. "I know a good place to hide the van."

So that's what they decided to do. But as luck would have it, they got stuck again on the way back to town. After that, a kindly law enforcement official who was passing by decided to give them a helping hand. Unfortunately, he got kind of suspicious because all three passengers seemed very nervous. He asked to look in the van. That's when the news came over his police scanner that there had been a big robbery in Snowflake Falls. And that's how Uncle Andy, Cookie Collito and Wally Whispers—who were dangerously close to becoming solid citizens—ended up back in jail.

As you can imagine, this left me in a rather awkward position. I guess I could have stayed with the Wingates for a while. But like my Uncle Andy said, there's something about this crazy town that makes you want to do the right thing against your better judgment.

So I ended up having a long talk with Mr. Wingate about pretty much every dishonest thing I had done while living in Snowflake Falls. I confessed to taking Harley's stretch limo for a ride and being a technical advisor to my uncle regarding the burglaries.

We talked over what I should do. And—to make a long story short—Mr. Wingate got me enrolled in a program for troubled youth. That's where I am now. On a farm near Vancouver, where I get up early to milk cows and clean out horse stalls and feed chickens. They are on what you call "the honor system" here. Between you and me, it would be the easiest thing in the world to break out of the place since security is very lax. In fact, I have thought about escaping many times. But—when it comes right down to it—I don't want to let the cows down. I guess my time at Top Kow made me very sentimental when it comes to the entire cow species.

Charlotte writes me very long letters that are almost like hearing her talk. She says that her dad is now giving

Biggie's a run for their money with a new business plan that includes staying open longer. I write her back and kid around, informing her that my hair has almost grown back to normal. George writes once in a while, too, keeping me up on what is happening at Top Kow. He says that when my time is up on the farm, he will gladly write me a recommendation for a job in the fast-food industry.

The biggest surprise is the dictated letter that I got from none other than Harley Howard—who got his new reader to write it out and send it to me. I expected Harley to be extra cranky about the whole robbery thing. But you know what? After a couple of pages of what you might call venting, he was surprisingly understanding. He said it took guts to turn myself in to Mr. Wingate like that. And that I had added a little zest to his life besides. He concluded his letter by saying that he hoped I would give total honesty a try. As he put it, "You might find it a refreshing change of pace."

I get to talk to Uncle Andy from prison once in a while. Like Wally and Cookie, he is back behind bars for the foreseeable future. The last time we conversed, I asked him if he thought I should have confessed my crimes to Mr. Wingate. "What can you do?" he said. "You're just like your mother." Then I told him I loved him, and he told me to not get kicked by a cow.

Uncle Andy told me that Cookie is working on an invention in prison. It is an anti-theft device especially designed for golf carts. Apparently, there is a golf-cart manufacturer who is thinking about paying him big bucks for his invention.

If it all works out, Cookie said we could all come and live with him in Arizona—which he refers to as "the golf course capital of the world." Of course, most of us have to wait until we're liberated from our current governmental responsibilities. I must say, I think about our Arizona dream a lot. I guess a lot depends on whether my Uncle Andy can lead a more honest lifestyle once his time in prison is done. Maybe I am being too optimistic. But I hope that we can all live together someday.

They work you pretty hard on this farm. But it is a good kind of work. Also, it gives you a lot of time to think about the sort of person you really want to be. I wrote a long letter to Old Maurice and he was very understanding. He even offered me a job as a dishwasher in his restaurant, after my time on the farm. It comes with a bonus of free room and board and the promise to look after me until things get a little more settled.

I told Old Maurice that I could get a recommendation from George. But he said I didn't need it. The whole thing sounds like a good deal to me. And I think I'm going to take him up on it, if Social Services gives us the okay. Old Maurice says he will do everything he can.

I think about my Uncle Andy a lot. I discovered that he had written a big letter of apology to Ms. Pendergast. And I think she has written back. I don't know if

Ms. Pendergast is the totally forgiving type, but I think the fact that she wrote back made Uncle Andy feel a little better. And, like Charlotte says, you never know what will happen when people start writing letters to each other.

A few days ago, I got a package from my uncle. It was a puzzle that came complete with a letter. The letter read *Dear Henry, This puzzle may help pass the time. I had it specially made for you at Christmas, but it was not ready in time. See you when I get out of jail. P.S. When you're working on the puzzle, pay close attention to the bottom part. It's tricky.*

It took me a long time to finish the puzzle, a very complicated nature scene with lots of blue sky. The bottom part was tricky but worth it. Because when I was all done, it read *I love you too. Uncle Andy.*

My uncle once told me that the best part of any puzzle is watching the picture slowly take shape. "Puzzles are a lot like life," he said. "Once everything fits into place, there's nothing left to discover." I think about that a lot when I'm lying in bed and trying to figure out why I miss Oscar's snores and Charlotte's nagging.

In a way, my Uncle Andy is right. Since the puzzle takes up a lot of space in my room, I should probably take the thing apart and put it back in the box. One of these days, I'll get around to doing just that.

ACKNOWLEDGMENTS

I could not have embraced with such complete happiness the sort of world this novel represents if it weren't for the early inspiration provided by three of my literary heroes. Accordingly, I'd like to pay homage to Damon Runyon, Lawrence Block and Donald E. Westlake for consistently nurturing my fascination with the comic potential of larceny.

I'm grateful to Jesse Finkelstein for her kind advice during the early stages of the manuscript. I'd like to thank everyone at Orca, with a lingering note of gratitude to Art Director Teresa Bubela. I'm especially indebted to my editor Sarah Harvey. Without her grace, insight and boundless affection for the manuscript, this would have been a very different book. Continued thanks for the unwavering support of my longtime agent Carolyn Swayze, along with a special shout-out to the intrepid Kris Rothstein. Lastly, I'd like to thank my family. Their abiding love and support is an integral part of this book.

JOHN LEKICH is a Vancouver-based author and free-lance writer whose work has appeared in such publications as *Reader's Digest*, the *Los Angeles Times* and *The Hollywood Reporter*. A former West Coast arts correspondent for *The Globe and Mail*, he is the recipient of ten regional and national magazine awards. His favorite interview subjects include Audrey Hepburn, George Plimpton, Garrison Keillor and silent screen star Lillian Gish.

John is the author of two previous young adult novels, *The Losers' Club* and *King of the Lost and Found*. He is currently working on a new novel.